Lord OF HER Dreams

Dream Series
book two

OLIVIA RITCH

PRAISE FOR DUKE OF HER DREAMS

An indescribably sweet book...five stars.

What follows, though, to my delight, were some nice twists and dangerous situations that threaten both their lives.

ISBN: 978-1-68046-702-4

Published by Satin Romance
An Imprint of Melange Books, LLC
White Bear Lake, MN 55110
www.satinromance.com

Published in the United States of America.

Cover Design by Caroline Andrus

To the people and pets at home who are constantly entertaining me.
Thank you for being my family.

PROLOGUE

September 2010

*M*ore than four months had passed with no trace of Kathryn Ragland. Christine Ragland looked for her missing sister across Alabama and the United States, to no avail. She cooperated with detectives and hired investigators, and they had all basically said they could do nothing more to find Kathryn. They would keep her case file open. Blah blah. The only good news she heard was thankfully, there were no murderers or criminals who had knowledge of her sister, and there were no unidentified bodies matching her description. Kathryn had simply vanished.

Today she was going to try an entirely different tack from the frustrating search she had made each previous day. She was going to retrace Kathryn's steps, as exactly as she could make out, on May 11th, the night she disappeared. The police told Christine that with so little to go on, her chances of finding Kathryn were slim. Kathryn had not left a clue as to her whereabouts. But Christine was not ever going to give up looking for her missing big sister.

Kathryn would never leave Christine on purpose. Never. Christine knew it in her bones. They were each other's only family but for cousins. They were inseparable. Christine was frantic. She was quite literally going out of her mind.

Kat hadn't taken her car or keys, no money had been spent from her bank account, and she hadn't told anyone she was leaving. Kidnapping was the only logical explanation the experts had developed, and Christine could fathom, to explain her sister's disappearance. But she had also, with no other explanations forthcoming, given in to the fiction that there was something else, some reason not logical, something no one had thought of that happened to Kathryn. Christy was desperate enough to consider anything.

If Kathryn Ragland was gone, it was because something terrible had happened, and Christine knew terrible things always left trails. Today she was going to follow Kathryn's trail.

She knew every step Kathryn had taken, to the minute. The police had been thorough. They just had run out of options. Someone was still assigned to her case even today, but no one was really actively looking for Kathryn Ragland, the social worker who had disappeared in the night from her suburban Birmingham, Alabama apartment.

Today, Christine was going to start at Kat's office and follow her entire schedule right through stopping at the little antique shop whose owner was the last person to have seen Kat. She had talked to Ms. Tilly several times and the elderly lady had been understanding, grandmotherly even, but had not shed any light on Kathryn's disappearance. Today, Christine was going in to shop only, just as she believed Kat had done.

Everyone at Kathryn's office watched her piteously. She hated being the cynosure of all eyes, but it couldn't be helped. Since she was a veterinarian, and this was a women's shelter, she did not actually have any meaningful work to do. Kathryn's case files had been given to others. There was nothing left of her sister's true work on the desk. But, she was determined to spend the entire work day in Kathryn's office, walking in her shoes as best she could. With rote movements, Christine stuffed flyers into envelopes, licked them shut and affixed stamps. She riffled through the few papers remaining on the desk, but for the most part, she simply passed the mind-numbing hours sitting wrapped in her morose thoughts at Kathryn's desk. At 5:15 p.m., the exact time Kathryn had departed, Christine slipped out to her car and drove toward the antique shop on Kathryn's route home she had visited so many times before in her fruitless search.

Christine sat for a few minutes in her car in the parking lot, willing her heart to regulate itself. She had become more and more anxious throughout the interminably long day, and now she felt like she was on the precipice of making a distinct step forward, instead of just marking the time.

Tilly was waiting for her by the door. "Come in, dear. I'm so glad to see you today. How are you doing?"

"Ms. Tilly, today's been so painful. I sat through her workday, dug through every sheet of paper in her desk, answered her few calls, sent out a mailing and nothing came to me. Nothing. Now I'm here to do everything she did after leaving work. There has to be some clue we've missed."

"You are such a faithful sister. It pains me so to see you suffer. I will walk with you and we will take her route through the store," Tilly took her elbow and steered Christine along a deliberate but winding route.

They made their way through the maze of crowded rooms filled with fanciful knick-knacks until they came to a small, familiar space in the back of the store. The moment she entered, the violent pang slammed into her. She staggered, sucking in her breath and Tilly tightened her grip on Christine's arm.

When Christine's breathing returned to normal a few moments later, Tilly spoke. "I've finally hung the paintings on the wall." Tilly pointed to the three small antique oils. "You know, your sister bought the only one with a woman in the portrait. Not like these others with only the English Lords."

Christine edged around the large table, leaning over the dresser against the wall to get a closer look at the artwork. She had seen them all before, but she looked as someone interested in buying. The red coated officer mounted on a striking black horse drew her eyes and she looked her question at Tilly. "Aye, dear, you can take it down."

Christine stared at the elegant face of the dark-haired man atop the magnificent horse and closed her eyes. Tilly had told her Kathryn had taken one of the portraits in the set. Had Kathryn been drawn to the portrait. Had it spoken to her or had she felt some connection? Why had she purchased the portrait?

Holding this portrait, Christine felt something. Her senses heightened. She tightened her grip on the lovely frame as she turned the picture over. There was no backing, any paper that had been there in the past was long ago torn away. There was nothing to tell her who had painted it or owned it, there were no words at all, but something tugged at her heart, her breathing suspended, the feelings so strong.

"I want you to have that. Take it home and remember." The gentle words comforted even as they deepened her sadness.

"Thank you, Ms. Tilly," Christine replied shakily. She had to keep holding the picture. It had somehow become vital to her to take it home to Kathryn's apartment and to anchor her for tonight.

❧

Christine left wordlessly and drove to Kathryn's place drowning in the fog of flooding memories. When she climbed into Kathryn's double bed, the dam of tears broke.

She did not know the painting she clutched was magic, that it had power over dreams, over place and time. She only knew somehow it made her feel connected to her sister. Weighed down with the fatigue of the truly sad, Christine fell deeply asleep. And in sleep, Christine dreamed of a dashing dark-eyed military officer with a midnight horse who was somehow the key to her search.

1

Herefordshire, England
September, 1816
Dawn

*M*atthew Drake needed to ride. He had not slept well, visions of creditors rushing to claim their debts pushing him, jostling with one another to take Worley away from him. He had tossed and turned finally resolving getting up and dressing for a ride was the only way to dispel the images and relax the nervous tension investing his entire body. Fully awake thanks to the cool morning air, Matthew strode briskly across the gravel toward the stable, wondering not for the first time how he was going to save his estate and keep himself out of debtor's prison.

The stable doors opened noiselessly thanks to hinges he had freshly oiled. They were among the very few doors to have been maintained at all on the estate. Half-light was enough for him to see to make straight for his horse's stall.

Opening his mouth to speak a welcome to the beast, Matthew's words caught in his throat. He lurched to a halt, his gaze fixed, mouth agape. He watched in both fascination and horror as tiny feet connected to luscious calves descended the rickety hayloft ladder. Lovely, lean thighs appeared next topped by a perfectly rounded female bottom marked by a single strap of green lace the color of the English Channel.

Transfixed by the sight of the lace, and the bottom, Matthew forgot to breathe and to worry about the unsafe ladder. But as the woman's back and shoulders came into view, the cascade of rich mahogany hair jolted him back to himself. If she turned around now and saw him just feet away, she would be scared witless. So, he gathered his senses enough to slip into the shadows of the closest open stall as his visitor reached the last rung and turned to view her surroundings.

"Ouch." She grunted as she stepped her bare feet onto the rough floor and turned fully into the dim stable. "Pokey straw. Straw!... What the..."

He watched the emotions flow from confusion to shock to disbelief across the woman's expressive face. Her huge eyes darted left and right but her body seemed frozen into immobility. With her rooted to the spot, generous breasts heaving, he could not help himself but be fixated on the vision she made.

Matthew also could not help but notice the green lace at the apex of her leanly muscled thighs and the way her navel peeked from just under her excuse for a shirt.

But even more, he was instantly sure he knew her. He could not help but see the young woman was as stunning as her elder sister Kathryn Ragland Stafford had described her. Matthew would have known this lady anywhere. Christine Mary Ragland was here in his barn, in his time. She had come for her sister.

Not until this moment had Matthew Dalton Anthony Drake, Baron Worley, believed Kathryn Stafford's story of being transported here by some unknown force. Not until now.

"Okay, breathe, Chris. Breathe. Now put one foot in front of the other. Ow...don't put one foot in front of the other. Damn, shit ...darn, I cussed. Pooh."

At her vivid expletive, Matthew's horse took offense and whickered, drawing Christine Ragland's attention. "Oh you. Look at you gorgeous...what are you?" She stepped toward the stall door and as she moved, Matthew did as well to keep out of his visitor's sight.

She took a crate and turned it on its side to peer into Knight's stall...her small but perfectly formed bottom traversed by the strip of lace jutting out while she peered. "Oh, you're a boy, are you? You are gorgeous." The woman, Christine, Matthew reminded himself, ran her small hands down his massive horse's snout and Knight whickered again. Matthew vividly imagined it was in pleasure at being caressed by such lovely, feminine hands.

Matthew closed his eyes and said a small prayer, for what he was doing was terribly wrong. If he was not so closely connected to Michael Stafford, having saved his life and Kathryn's each at least once, he knew Michael would have killed him on the spot for his thoughts about the lovely, tiny woman in his stable. Matthew had stared for much too long now to suddenly announce himself. If he devised a retreat and then returned loudly a short time later, he could make his presence known.

At that moment, his best friend's sister-in-law leaned more fully over the side of the stall to continue crooning at Knight. "Oh, you are a magnificent midnight horse, aren't you? Oh yes, you whickered again at that. Is your name Midnight?" Close enough, it was Knight. "Until I learn differently, I'm calling you Midnight and boy I am so glad to see you. You're not going to believe what happened to me."

He should have slipped away right then, but he had to know what she was going to tell his horse and, unwisely, he was still mesmerized by her bottom and the tiny lace stretched across it. "Midnight," she breathed before continuing, "My sister went missing last May, and I have looked for her everywhere." Christine stroked his horse's neck almost absently as she wove her tale for all the barn's occupants.

"Last night or yesterday or well...the last time I remember, I traced every step she took. Can you believe that I found a painting of a horse just like you and now that must be why I feel like you and I are together in the most vivid dream of my life." She stopped to breathe and let out a small sigh this time. "It's not really a dream though is it Midnight? I've gone somewhere, haven't I?" She stopped again. He fervently prayed she would continue spinning the fabulous yarn.

"Don't feel like you have to answer. I know it. The only thing I am holding on to right now to keep from freaking out is that maybe Kathryn is here too, and I can take her home where she belongs."

Home where she belongs? Kathryn Ragland Stafford is where she belongs, here with her husband, carrying his child. She was not going anywhere.

Matthew had to get away before Christine Ragland found him ogling her and before he spoke up to argue with her accidentally. And, he was not ready to compromise her which he surely would if they were found together in the barn, her clearly nearly naked.

He needed to learn more of her story and he wanted to be able to talk to her face-to-face, not like a peeping Tom. He certainly couldn't talk to her as she was now. Matthew hoped she would find some riding gear in the trunk in the tack room and put it on before he came back.

Taking a cautious step toward the door, he moved with the skill of one who had avoided danger his entire life and made his escape without drawing her attention. Then Matthew Drake leaned against the outer stable wall and breathed heavily as if he had escaped a fate worse than death. His life was already complicated. Debts of myriad amounts to so many, caused by his wastrel brother Sebastian's poor handling of cards and drink had all but broken the estate while

Matthew had been gone on the Continent. Matthew had been the second son, a military prodigy, and had come home to virtual poverty.

Now he had Christine Ragland who, according to her elder sister, was training or had been trained as a veterinarian, whose riding skills reputedly matched his own and whose stunning beauty had not been exaggerated, standing in the flesh in his barn, in his life. However, would a cavalry officer with little to no experience with women and not a farthing to his name cope?

He needed Michael Stafford, now.

Matthew surged from his resting place toward the house, jerking the front door hard enough to startle his elderly housekeeper. "Mrs. Soggs, will you please send Hunter to me," he asked the trusty retainer upon gaining the entrance hall.

The bare walls were testament to his impoverished state. The only room Matthew had been able to devise into some semblance of gentility to help him keep up any appearance of wealth was his study. Soon, at the rate the notes of hand were being presented to him for payment, he was sure even the study would be bare of his family's possessions. To stave off the worst of the creditors and to pay the wages for his housekeeper and her grandson, he sold his heirlooms one at a time. The two were virtually his only staff and he hoped he could manage, but then he had discovered the mountain of debt his brother had amassed in a ridiculous string of gambling and extravagancies.

"M'Lord, Grand said you'd sent fer me."

"Yes, Hunter, I need you to get a note over to His Grace at Hawthorne and I need you to go as fast as you can." Matthew was quickly scratching on the paper as the boy stood ready to bolt.

"Yes, M'Lord, I can run there in a trifle, but I could ride...." He looked hopeful.

"I know you can, run that is. I just cannot get Knight out now though. And one other thing," Matthew cautioned. The young man looked his question.

"Yes, sir?"

"Try to see His Grace alone without Her Grace."

"Oh, Aye, I see. Secret message?"

"Yes, a very big secret, Hunter." A very small big secret.

Before Michael arrived, Matthew knew he had to see Christine at least passably dressed, even if he had to surprise her in the process to accomplish the feat. He sucked in a breath and strode for his bedchamber. Surely, he had something she could put on. In the end, he decided that one of his shirts, if matched with a blanket, would cover enough of her for them to get her decently into the house. He grabbed the items and headed for the stairs. "Mrs. Soggs?"

"Yes, my lord?"

"We have a visitor," he declared, watching her reaction.

"A visitor? I didn't see anyone ride up," the perceptive woman commented drily.

"No, you wouldn't have. This one has stowed away in our hayloft."

"The hayloft? Why ever for?" Her eyes were round.

"I have no idea but I'm on my out to introduce myself. When His Grace arrives, send him that way."

"His Grace? Ye've sent for the Duke?" He knew she must think him ready for Bedlam.

"Yes, I need him. It's complicated."

"Well, yes sir. Although I just can't imagine." She humphed and shuffled to let him out the door.

"Aye." He could imagine a lot, he already had.

Matthew stomped loudly up to the stable door and then banged it open with enough force to startle Knight, then apologized to the horse to be sure the woman heard him. "Ahhh...helloooo, who's there?" his errant visitor called in an unsure voice.

"Lord of this estate, Baron Worley," he called to the voice.

"I...I...I'm Christine. Can you stay where you are for just a minute?"

"I am not moving."

As she emerged from behind Knight's stall, Christine Ragland was buttoning the flap of a pair of riding pants. She must have scavenged them from among the discards. Matthew had thought her stunning naked, but dressed, she was equally potent. Her sister had said that where she herself was freckled, Christine had a flawless face. While the Duchess' hair was multicolored, Christine's was a rich deep brown with auburn undertones and where Kathryn's eyes were hazel, Christine's were pure green. Matthew had sometimes wondered about meeting a mahogany-haired, green-eyed Ragland beauty but had never fully envisioned a creature, a woman, this gorgeous.

The eyes were indeed as stunning as Kathryn had described. Christine's were the color of flawless emeralds and large as saucers as they were staring at him in disbelief.

"Miss Christine? Do I...know you?" Matthew asked still trapped in her befuddled green gaze. He watched her move toward him, her eyes now narrowing to study him. Time stretched.

"Probably not," she said after long silent minutes.

"I'm sorry?"

"You asked if you knew me. My answer is that I doubt you do. I'm Christine Ragland and, actually, I find myself totally surprised to be in your barn."

"It is a rather interesting development for me as well to walk in to find a woman here. Especially one with a foreign accent who is..."

"Is what?"

"Ahem, dressed like that."

Matthew regretted the words the moment he said them because Christine flung her arms across her middle to cover her breasts and stain colored her cheeks. He had not meant to alarm her, but she had obviously realized he had had a very good look at her protruding nipples. "I ah, am sort of without..."

"I'm sorry Miss, that was terribly rude of me. I happen to have an extra shirt in my saddle bags. I thought...I might need a change. You can borrow it if you like."

He eased into the stall, grabbed the shirt he had stashed, kicking himself for a fool, by embarrassing her so. He straightened and wiped the frustration from his face to greet her with an easy smile.

She reached with one hand for the shirt keeping the other tightly pressed to her chest. He stepped close enough to reach her outstretched hand and his breath caught in his chest, once again. Up close to her like this, Matthew could smell Christine. Although she had probably slept in his hay, the faint scent of bananas and lady powder clung to her. And she smelled slightly of sweat and musk. Her feminine odor tantalized his senses and he eased out of her reach to give her room to breathe as well.

"Th—thank you."

She shrugged into the shirt and tied the tails of it into a knot at her waist. In his loose shirt, the sleek riding pants and standing small and barefoot, she looked like all the trouble he knew she would be.

Matthew shook his head to clear it and to form his question, "Now that is done, would you care to tell me how you came to be in my stable?"

"Well, it's not that I would or wouldn't care to... I just really don't know. I think I might have an idea but it's so crazy, I can't quite bring myself to give it voice just yet."

"You might be surprised at how understanding I can be," Matthew responded wryly.

"You might be understanding, but I'm not ready to try it yet. Can we just go with I'm a lost American in search of her sister?"

"That's certainly plausible. You probably are lost and you certainly sound like you could be American."

"Since we both agree I'm lost, can you tell me where I am? You said this is Worley? And you haven't yet said who you are."

"I apologize. I am Matthew Drake and yes, Worley is my estate. You're in Herefordshire, England." Matthew watched her eyes widen noticeably at that pronouncement.

"Since I've only seen the barn, I can't be sure, but everything looks a little…"

"Run down?"

"I was going to say historical." He knew what she really meant but allowed the moment to pass so as not to cause her any distress.

"You could say it that way. My estate does need some care. I am embarrassed to say it has not been well attended in my absence."

"Where have you been?"

"The Continent. Spain, France, Portugal, Belgium," he replied in the same tone.

"For how long?"

"Until the war ended late last year."

"Last year being…?"

"1815."

"1815?"

Christine's gorgeous emerald eyes became once again the size of saucers and she began to shake and sway as if she might faint. Matthew reached for her and as he pressed her small body into his, the wave of desire that flooded his senses threatened to bring him down on top of her. He leaned her back into the wall by Knight's stall and smoothed a lock of hair from her face.

He knew she was out of her time, that she was from sometime, somewhere in the future. She would be shocked to hear she really had come back here. Christine would be even more shocked to learn that they all had expected her because her big sister had preceded her.

ichael Stafford crested the rise on the back of his favorite mount Fury, drawing rein in the shade of the tree at the edge of the bridle path just north of Worley. He could see the figures leading Matthew Drake's stallion out of the stable. Matthew was accompanied by a small, familiar looking woman. Even from this distance, Michael recognized the fluid movements, the manner, and the small frame, and immediately knew why he had been summoned with all urgency to Worley. His Kathryn had described the girl in detail, so many times. Now, seeing Christine Ragland in the flesh, crooning to Matthew's mount seemed natural, destined, nothing unusual. That she was here surprised him not at all. That she might try to take his wife away with her back to wherever she rode in from scared him to the core of his being.

Michael had no doubt the girl, his beloved wife's sister, was searching for Kathryn. They were close. They loved each other as he loved his sister Cassandra. He had hauled Cassandra bodily out of her father-in-law's house. He had no doubt love had the power to propel people to great feats but fortunately, tiny Christine Ragland would not be able to haul Michael's pregnant wife anywhere.

His heart constricted at the thought of Kathryn, their child growing inside her, weak and forced to rest. She had not yet recovered her strength, certainly not enough to run away. But what would she do when she found out Christine was here? Michael would not even contemplate Kathryn's leaving him. The only option was to convince Christine to stay or compel her.

And if Christine remained with them, Kathryn would be over the moon with joy. It would make this awful confinement she was suffering bearable, even joyous. He had no doubt Christine could provide hour upon hour of distraction for his beloved. But for now, they would proceed with caution. He would do nothing to upset the fragile state of his still much too thin and weak wife. Her health and that of their child's, was his only concern.

Turning Fury's head in the direction of Matthew's stable, Michael galloped determinedly toward his newly found sister-in-law.

Christine saw the rider emerge from the stand of trees in perfect harmony with his horse, his dark hair and the tails of his jacket flowing in the breeze. The beautiful brown beast he rode was huge and barrel-chested to hold such a large man. Upon reaching them, the man dismounted with a fluid grace that belied his tremendous size and when he spoke, the voice was even more of a surprise. "Matthew, you have a visitor?"

Her first thought was he smiled with his whole face and her second thought was the smile was lethal. Then he faced her with an inquiring raise of his eyebrows at his friend. Oh my!

"Yes, Your Grace, may I present Miss Christine Ragland? Miss Ragland, Michael Stafford, His Grace, the Duke of Asterleigh."

"Miss Ragland, charmed. My servants are the only ones who call me 'His Grace.' I would welcome you to call me Michael." Your sister does.

"Christine."

"Pardon?"

"You can call me Christine," she announced with what bravado she could muster. This was a real live Duke!

"Wonderful." He turned to the estate owner, whose name was Matthew. She was not sure what to make of the odd expression she caught on his regal face, but she was sure some unspoken communication passed between the two men. The brief interlude gave her the opportunity to study both of them together and she thought she had never seen two such imposing men standing so close to her. Michael was huge while Matthew was much leaner, more like someone who rode often, but he was as tall. Their faces and the way they held their shoulders screamed nobility.

If they noticed her close inspection, they did not comment as they shook hands and clapped shoulders. She sneaked another look and recalled Matthew's boyish smile lit up his handsome face and showed off his high cheekbones and the cleft in his chin, while Michael's smile had been lethally charming. Matthew reminded her of a soap star, lean and chiseled and perfect—someone ideal to feature on a poster for a teenager's wall.

She was terribly grateful that neither man resembled her sandy haired, freckled, faithless Adonis look-alike father. While Kathryn unfortunately did have her coloring from their Father, Christine got her own from their mom. Michael's hair was as black as his eyes, scraping his shoulders in disarray from his ride. Matthew's hair was perfectly groomed, and almost her color brown, and his eyes were as dark as Michael's. Neither of them resembled her scoundrel dad and for that she was grateful.

Christine thought of the painting of the cavalry officer she had been given by Ms. Tilly and decided Matthew was exactly the sort to have been in the cavalry. If Matthew had been cavalry, then Michael was more like a foot soldier, probably someone who lugged cannons on his back or managed with some other equally huge and heavy weaponry.

～

"Miss Ragland, what brings you to us?" the Duke who wanted her to call him Michael asked, shaking her from her fascinating study of their aristocratic features.

A wormhole, a time machine. "A quest."

"A quest? Intriguing. Do tell." The Duke raised that inquiring brow at her again and shifted his large frame to face her directly.

"I'm looking for my sister. My older sister. She disappeared more than three months ago, and I retraced her steps yesterday and ended up here."

"You retraced her steps? Where did you come from and how did you get here?" He asked it in a tone she suspected he thought was mildly inquiring. It was not. He was too big and too male and too... close for mild.

"That's...complicated." But of course he waited for more of an answer. She was still not ready to give one. If she hadn't wanted to with one nobleman staring down at her, she certainly wasn't more inclined now that she was all but surrounded by them. "I'm sure I could not recall my route now that I have gotten...lost. I need some time to..." *figure out how I time traveled back almost 200 years* "...to get my bearings and get back on my sister's trail." Even to her ears, that was too weak an answer.

"And what of your quest...if you find her?" His inquiry was once again as mild as he seemed capable of, but Christine detected a note of something else in his voice. Had it been doubt or concern?

"First, I'll probably fall on my knees with joy, then I'll hug her until we both cry then I'll try to figure out how to go about getting us both back to where we belong."

She could not believe that these two Lords of the land were regarding her with all seriousness and not laughing at her. In fact, she had watched Michael's expression for any sign that he thought she was up to no good and he had been surprisingly indulgent. Her unease turned to relief as she realized he seemed simply interested, not judging, or questioning her arrival into their lives. Looking at Matthew for confirmation, she saw the same acceptance. Christine would not question the luck that had allowed her to breeze through her explanations without having to tell these men that she had fallen asleep and woken here in...wherever she really was.

"We need to get you more settled with us, with proper clothes and I daresay you are hungry?" Matthew added as he began to move them all toward the manor home. She had noticed the stately old house just up the hill from the stables where she had spent her waking hour meeting the beautiful black stallion and his equally beautiful master.

"Starving actually. I fell asleep without dinner," Christine admitted, now realizing how true the statement was. Her stomach rumbled at that exact moment, confirming her state to the men, causing all of them to chuckle.

"Matthew, I believe there are some garments at Hawthorne that could be spared. I will send them over straightaway upon my return," the Duke offered as they walked.

"Oh, wow, no, I mean...don't go to any trouble for me. I can just wear these," Christine looked down at her borrowed clothes.

"Miss Ragland?" She swung her gaze toward Matthew as he spoke. "I assure you, you cannot just wear what you have on."

"But it's fine..."

"Miss...Christine. I will send garments. We have plenty to spare and I daresay, you will realize you cannot sport boy's togs in front of the servants. And certainly not in front of guests for it will not be in any way considered proper. And I will send assistance. You will need a dresser to assist you." When someone as large and intimidating as the Duke looked just now, spoke as he was doing, Christine found it easy to concede. "Lord Worley, may I see you in your study on another matter?"

"Will you excuse us, Miss Ragland? I will leave you to Mrs. Soggs." Matthew turned a bright smile on her and she knew they were going off to talk about her. That wasn't surprising. What was surprising was how routinely they had acted. There had not been nearly enough doubt in their manners. Indeed, they had believed her far too easily. Something was definitely up.

"It is quite remarkable to have her here in the flesh, is it not?" Matthew opined.

"It is at that. And after my reaction to the explanations Kathryn gave me at the beginning of our acquaintance about her appearing here out of the clear blue, thinking as I did it all was pure drivel, I am just grateful I did not treat her with contempt."

"You are fortunate you were able to work through it. And how is the lovely Duchess today?"

"Strengthening, but...this will be a shock. Probably a good shock unless Miss Ragland has designs on their returning home. If that is the case, the answer is no. I will do whatever I have to do to end that discussion on the spot."

"This one seems less eager to depart than your Kathryn. I remember the grand chase within days of her arrival and I think this one may be a bit more grounded."

"Matthew, you are right about that but remember, Kathryn was worried about Miss Ragland. She was frantic to get back to her and had no idea what was happening. Miss Ragland knows her sister is missing, and she probably realizes this is some next stage in her search, so she is open to any circumstance. Although I cannot truly imagine what must be going through her head."

Michael moved to the window and pulled the curtain back from the glass. "She is as exquisite as my wife has described her."

Matthew joined him at the window and recalled the woman whose perfectly shaped bottom was marked indelibly on his brain. He could not look at or think of her without the image of that narrow strip of green lace and the imminently squeezable globes of her bottom coming to the fore. "I never believed your wife, I am sorry to say, but I did listen, and wondered. She is amazingly lovely...." His voice trailed off. He had no right to even look at her, much less imagine.

"She would make you an excellent wife."

"Hah, now you are just being cruel, eh?"

"Cruel?"

"You know full well I will not have any wife while this estate is being restored. I have nothing to offer."

"You are wrong my friend. You are a wonderful catch even if your fortune is somewhat depleted. She would be the perfect partner in your venture ...with her background."

Yes, Christine Ragland would be a perfect partner...for someone. It would not be him. Miss Christine Ragland would be long married before Matthew was solvent enough to take on a wife and family. "Are you going to come get her soon? She can't stay here."

"She has to stay here. I can't bring her home with me yet?"

"So, you are going to have me compromise her into marrying me. That's low for you."

"Matthew, petulance does not become you. I will send one of the Primble girls to you and clothes and we will form our plan. I might enlist Cass..."

"Michael..." He took in a slow deep breath. "I'm not the solution to this problem for you."

"Matthew. This is not only my problem. She is as much your responsibility since she made her appearance here as she is mine, and we both want to stay in as good graces as we can with both her and Kathryn. We will figure this out together. Just get her into a gown as soon as you bloody well can and whatever you do, don't admit any visitors."

"Visitors? You can't be serious?"

"As soon as Mrs. Stogwell knows you are settling in and Mrs. Pembroke…" his voice trailed away.

"Bloody hell."

"Let's drink to agreeing on that."

"Hallthorpe? Where is Her Grace?

"She is still abed, Your Grace."

"Good. Please send Eleanor Primble to me. My study."

"Right away." With that, Michael's butler was off to fetch Kathryn's maid. Michael strode the hall to his study and dropped into the chair. He hoped to accomplish this mission before the duchess awoke.

"Your Grace?"

"Miss Primble, please join me." Ellie stepped into his study, a person who had become not only a trusted ally but so much a part of their lives after just a few weeks in his household. "I have need of your utmost discretion."

"Aye, Your Grace. You can count on me."

"Yes, I know. Her Grace's sister has arrived." Ellie's eyes widened, and she opened her mouth to speak but Michael held up one hand to forestall any explanation, not allowing the much too intuitive maid to change the subject. He watched her take in every aspect of his plans.

"I don't see any problem with that, Your Grace. Beth is here today and can take a few things with her this morning and we can ready another batch for this evening after Her Grace retires tonight."

"Very good. You are dismissed."

Ellie turned to go but he could see she just couldn't hold her tongue on one small point of his plan. "She will be angry when she learns she has been denied this reunion."

Michael had never felt the weight of his choice more as he closed his eyes. "I know, it isn't forever, but Miss Primble...I need to know more before I throw her into the situation."

He steeled his last words and Ellie got the message, effacing herself and slipping from the room. His wife's maid cared about her mistress and understood why he was keeping her sister from her. Michael had spoken true, this denial wouldn't be forever, just until he could be sure that he was in complete control.

For that, he needed to continue his plan to shore up Matthew's financial situation. The sooner Christine Ragland was comfortably married to his oldest friend the better. He dashed off notes to Julian Thornton, Earl of Weatherford, and Colin Hamilton, his two silent partners in settling the crushing debt left to Matthew Drake, by his elder brother Sebastian. The Baron had left his heir up the River Tick and someone was purchasing the estate's debts as fast as he and his partners were. There was no doubt that the other purchaser was up to no good.

From atop his horse on the low rise, he could just make out the figures moving in and about the Worley stables. The rider was sure his eyes were not deceiving him. There was a long-haired visitor shoveling hay just outside the stable door. The master would probably not be pleased to know that this person looked very much like a woman. Women always posed extra problems.

3

*M*iss Ragland?"

"Christine."

"Christine. A maid has just arrived from Hawthorne with some clothes. May I invite you inside to find a room and get freshened up?" Matthew said.

"Sure, that's great. Thank you."

"And when you are dressed, you will please join me in the dining room? I expect you are famished and ready to break your fast."

"Starving, actually. I think I mentioned I fell asleep without eating."

"We cannot have guests starving on their arrival days."

"That implies they might starve other times?"

His smile was wide, his teeth straight and white as he absorbed her quip. "Touche', Christine. Never say it. Just that you have indeed arrived hungry and we haven't offered you anything." Matthew turned at the rustling skirts behind him and gestured the woman forward. "Ah, Mrs. Soggs, this is Miss Ragland. She will be staying a few..."

"Hours?" She looked at him hopefully.

"Days."

"No, I just need to get changed and then figure out my next steps. I won't be staying."

Matthew didn't argue. There was, in fact, not going to be a debate. Christine wasn't leaving, and he would be preventing any attempt on her part. The confounding woman was fortunate he was a patient man because her matter-of-fact tone about leaving so soon would have angered other less controlled gentlemen—some of whom were his closest friends. As it was, Christine was trying his control merely by being here. Of course, the discussion of clothes and freshening up had made his imaginings so much worse.

There was a definite disadvantage to remaining a virgin at his horribly advanced age of eight and twenty. His imagination for salacious details was entirely too well used. Matthew wondered if he would even be able to watch her eat, with that perfectly formed mouth...

From her first, distant glimpse Christine thought the house was charming with its stacked stone foundation and glorious windows, gables, and rooflines. But as she drew nearer, studying the house, she saw signs of neglect and an odd lack of ornamentation. Something about the house looked almost...bare.

She heard Matthew speaking in low tones with Mrs. Soggs and took the opportunity to study her surroundings. He addressed Mrs. Soggs and she was drawn out of her brown study of the bare walls. "Would you show her to a room?"

"Yes, my lord. This way, miss."

Christine hadn't missed the sidelong glance the woman had given her boss.

Christine had the odd feeling that she had already lived this scene, that she had been exactly here, attended by the elderly housekeeper while the elegant gentleman waited below. She shivered at the palpable sense of déjà vu.

"Maid's here, miss. She's waiting for you in your room."

Christine followed the slow-moving woman who she assumed was the housekeeper up a wide flight of stairs with worn treads, past bare walls, where they emerged onto a landing with equally unadorned walls and several closed doors. Only one stood open and sounds of activity came from within.

Christine passed Mrs. Soggs, stepping over the threshold into a room only slightly more charming than the rest of the near-empty house. She took in the bed with fresh-looking pillows, the one candle glowing on a dresser holding a few bottles and one silver brush. The presence of the surprisingly young woman dressed in a maid's uniform in the room suggested they were going to a lot of trouble for their surprise guest.

"Ah, miss, I am Beth, and I'm fair pleased to meet you."

"Call me Christine, please. And I'm pleased to meet you too."

"Well, I can see ye're in dire need of a bath and some, er...lady's clothes. I'll just go down and ask after that water, then I'll come help you out of your boy's togs and..."

"I think I can handle undressing. I'll just strip out of these dirties and grab that robe if that's okay with you.

"Ha yes, miss that suits just fine. I'll be right back. Mrs. Soggs'll show me the way." She didn't really know why the maid was laughing and shaking her head as she left. Or what the murmuring of the two women meant.

Beth the maid was remarkably talented with a hairbrush. Christine remembered nights of beauty makeovers when she and Kathryn were girls growing up and that most had resulted in messy faces and tangled hair. She spoke again to cover the accompanying pang of sadness she felt. "You're really good at that. I can't remember the last time someone twisted my hair up on my head and made it look good."

"Oh miss, yours is so glorious. It's not really brown is it, more red than not."

"It's definitely a mix." She did not want to veer into the subject of her heritage. "So, Beth, you live around here?"

"'I'm from just outside the village, Wilton, that is. But I spend more time at Hawthorne than home these days."

"Hawthorne?"

"It's the Duke's estate, miss."

"The Duke I met? What's it like living with a Duke?"

Beth laughed a little. "It's not actually like living with the Duke. It's just living in the Duke's manor. I sew mostly. Don't see His Grace that often."

Christine wondered if she should ask the maid about Kathryn. What if she was here in this village somewhere? It wouldn't be any more unbelievable than Christine's own journey. But, if Kathryn was hiding or had not been found by decent people, she might need her secret identity. Christine decided it was too soon to broach the subject of her lost sister.

"You can take another look now, miss."

"I hope you'll call me Christine since I am calling you Beth."

"Very well. Turn around."

"Oh my gosh. Who is that?"

"Who indeed? You look amazing. Lord Worley's going to be besotted as soon as he sets eyes on you."

"I'm not trying to beset Lord Worley."

"You won't have to try."

"Great," she humphed.

Beth drew Christine to her feet which were now decidedly rooted to the spot. Christine could not fathom going out looking as she did.

Dressed in an ancient ball gown with ringlets of hair trailing down her neck and strands of jewels strung through the tight braids on top, she looked like someone out of time. But she was someone out of time, wasn't she? No, she wanted to believe she was still a regular woman, who rode horses and wore blue jeans as her primary mode of dress. She was certainly not a debutante in a historical romance novel. But, the Christine Ragland staring back at her in the long mirror was exceptionally...beautiful. Well. "Go on miss, you are quite ready,"

"You say that I'm ready, but I feel like...an imposter."

"That's what Her Grace...that's what a lot of ladies say the first time they get a maid to do their hair and gown," Beth stuttered, shifting away from Christine to tidy the dresser.

Christine wondered very much who "Her Grace" was that Beth clearly did not mean to mention. The girl knew something. Christine just hoped she was not walking into a strange trap like that other woman. And she was sure she was still awake. This adventure was not a dream.

Taking the stairs more carefully than would have been necessary in her favorite flip flops, Christine in fact glided regally down to a waiting host whose back was to her. When Matthew Drake, Lord Worley, turned to face Christine fully, his gasp was audible. She had never heard a man do that before and felt a little feminine satisfaction at causing that kind of reaction in a man whose outward beauty was so startling she had barely been able to be within three feet of him without heart palpitations.

In fact, Matthew Drake was a certifiable hottie. Who could forget the amazingly long lean legs or the narrow waist with not even one tiny inch of flab? Christine loved long arms and wide flat chests. Matthew Drake's were the best examples of both she had ever seen. But it was his absolutely perfect face that caused Christine to stifle a corresponding gasp. In his midnight blue evening coat, Matthew

Drake looked like a...a...she couldn't think what. When the object of her imaginings smiled, she realized what he looked like, an innocent devil. If there was such a thing.

It didn't make sense how she had come to the conclusion that Matthew Drake was oxymoron personified but she was sure that's exactly what he was. Matthew looked smart and sweet, powerful and vulnerable, wealthy but impoverished, strong yet gentle, perfectly poised but nervous as a teenager. Matthew was a conundrum. An exquisite conundrum who was smiling and reaching for her hand and Christine had to be careful not to fall the last few steps into an ignominious heap at his feet.

"Miss Ragland, you look...divine."

"You do too."

"Well...thank you," he sniffed, obviously not sure what to make of Christine's compliment. And she was sure she saw a faint blush.

"We will dine in the large dining room but the seats have been set closer so you do not feel you have to yell across the expanse."

"I can't see myself sitting fifty places away and trying to talk, so thank you for...arranging it."

With this woman on his arm, Matthew almost forgot his problems. The threat of impending debtor's prison fell away, transportation to Botany Bay almost forgotten. The small incidents of vandalism that had been plaguing the stables, the complete lack of staff and the methodical dismantling of his family's possessions were almost consigned to the devil as he gazed down into the brilliant green eyes and perfectly heart-shaped face of his stunning guest. "How did you find the accommodations?" Asking an innocuous question was the only way Matthew was going to keep from stumbling at the beauty's feet.

"My room? It was very nice, thank you again."

"And the maid?"

"Beth, you mean?"

"I do believe that was the young woman's name," her openness bringing a lift to his lips.

"Oh, she's great. Honestly didn't know what to make of having someone actually put me into the dress but..." Matthew noticeably blushed at that. "Was I not supposed to mention getting dressed?"

"I am sorry. I shouldn't have let your remark embarrass me." Now he was actually being gauche. "So having a maid dress you is a new experience?"

"Totally. Although I do have an older sister who delights in tormenting me about my clothes. But it's definitely not the same."

Suddenly desperate to change the subject now Christine mentioned Kathryn again, he latched onto one sure to snag her interest. "So, you are a horsewoman?"

"Not so much a horse woman, as an animal lover. I've just graduated vet school."

He knew these details of her life, but they nonetheless made for a wonderful diversion from the one he would not discuss. "You are a veterinary doctor?"

"Yeah, did I not mention that already?"

"I do not think I would have missed it."

"Sorry. Kat says I'm bad about assuming..." Her sentence unfinished, Matthew hoped that both Christine and Kathryn would indeed be able to forgive him and Michael for this period of deception once they were reunited. Christine's green eyes clouded to dark moss at the mention once again of her supposed missing sister. "I...I...dammit...oh my gosh, I'm so sorry for cussing."

Reaching for her hand, Matthew did what felt so natural and necessary at the moment, bringing her tiny digits to his mouth, and then letting the caress linger longer than propriety suggested. When the same lovely eyes that had clouded with sadness moments ago now widened with awareness and glowed a dark evergreen, Matthew knew he was not going to be able to dismiss his attraction to this woman. Christine's well-being was already becoming essential to him.

Having once again released her hand to her own keeping, Matthew gestured to the seat Thrasher, another new addition to his household, was holding for her. The young man assisted her then moved to the side board to serve the meal. Matthew turned his attention to the soup Thrasher had placed before each of them. Michael insisted on sending Beth for Christine and Thrasher to attend in the house. Matthew also believed he knew of the hardship it was for the young man to be separated from his love Ellie, the Duchess's maid. Well-trained and conscious of the regard his master afforded him, the footman bowed and removed himself to retrieve the next course.

"How do you find the soup?" Matthew asked.

"I find it...marvelous."

The smile Christine bestowed on him as she made the pronouncement sent a fierce wave of desire crashing through him. Unused to such a strong reaction to a simple smile, Matthew dropped his spoon. The utensil hit the china dish on a weak spot breaking it sending a wave of soup across the table, and surprising Christine into exclaiming and knocking over her wineglass. As the red beverage mixed with the heavier cream, a disgusting flow of pinkish liquid oozed ominously toward his guest's lap. Laughing with the disaster of their combined spills, Christine shrugged and with remarkable dexterity, positioned her bowl to catch the mixture as it slopped over into her lap.

"Thrasher, we have had an accident, of sorts." Matthew addressed the footman who had rushed back into the room at the sounds of consecutive breakages. "I believe we will need to repair somewhere else to eat."

"Lord...Worley...Matthew? Would it really be a problem to umm, eat like in the kitchen or the...do you have a breakfast nook?" Christine said.

Abandoning Thrasher to the disaster he and Christine had made at the dining table, Mathew took her hand and towed Christine toward the kitchen with all speed. "Cook will not be pleased we've invaded her space. You will need to charm her with that lovely smile of yours," he teased as they stopped just outside the door.

Her conspiratorial whisper had him leaning close where he got a nose full of fragrant curls. "Is she nice or what is the word, a gargon?"

"Aye, she's not exactly nice but since me, my brother and my pack of friends ran tame in this house as children, coming through and stealing tarts, she has a soft spot for me."

"Then maybe you're the one who needs to give her the winning smile." He laughed fully for the first time in days and pushed the door open to the not completely warm welcome of his aggrieved cook.

She was not making progress. Not in her search for her sister or in aiding her own departure. She had made great progress in finding Matthew Drake charming, irresistible, and ridiculously handsome and she was sure all of that was part of his intended distraction. Oh, she was all but certain Matthew Drake knew more than he had told her. His acceptance of her story of appearing from a dream was just a little too quick. She didn't even believe it, how had he come to so quickly accept her tale. His staff's ability to produce clothes that fit her on a moment's notice—when they had so few obvious resources was a sign, of something. She had not yet gotten all the pieces in place. But, as she also sensed a wariness about her presence, she did not expect any of them to answer her direct questions.

She had imagined interrogating the maid Beth and discarded the idea as soon as it had formed. Beth was not going to tell her anything substantive. She had to find out on her own what this household was hiding.

The hallway was relatively dark, being lit by just one candle. She remembered the landing and the stairs and had paid attention to the door to the Master's study. She found it shut and wasted no time on examining her decision. Her conscience was clear. Kathryn was missing, Matthew knew more than he was letting on and she wanted answers.

She did not light the desk lamp but did flick open the curtain on the closest French door. The fabric was old and worn and she feared it would come off in her hands. That would be a dead giveaway. But, Christine also was quite sure men like Matthew Drake would know if someone had rifled through their desks. She would have to be very careful not to touch anything that did not look relevant.

Of course, she had not expected the desk to be locked. Locked! How would she ever search it? "Looking for this?" She whirled to face the man attached to that low, darkly menacing voice. Matthew stood in the door with the half-light from the hall casting his austere face in shadows, a key dangling on a chain cinched at his waist.

He moved as quietly as she expected a stalking jungle cat would. He set the key on the desk and slid it toward her. "What are you looking for, Miss Ragland? What do you hope to find?"

"I ah..." Think. Why couldn't she think? "I wanted to know..."

"Yes?" He lifted one eyebrow in that arrogant manner she suspected intimidated servants and subordinates into quiet. Gone was the affable dinner partner. In his place was the deadly serious nobleman.

So she gathered her wits and faced him fully unwilling to be intimidated. "I wanted to know if my sister..." She stopped, breathed, and started again in a stronger voice. "I...I think you know something about her." There, she had said it firmly enough he would see she would accept no further stalling.

"You believe I know something. What do I know, Miss Ragland?" His almost lethal purr shook her resolve, but she was now determined to get some, any answers.

"I believe you know where she is. You and your friends who have been so very helpful today. Where is she?"

He did not answer but moved toward the desk, bending on one knee to slip the key he had taunted her with into the lock. The drawer slid soundlessly and as he reached in, she sucked in a tight breath. "You think I'm going to draw out a pistol, Miss Ragland?" he asked in that purr with the added mocking edge of a man pushed too far.

"No, I...no. I just want to know."

He handed her the portrait of...himself. She stared into his handsome face, she knew now was so very well captured by the artist and ran her finger across the frame she had also held in another time and place. He was still dressed in his regimentals, the upright posture familiar. This time, she felt the paper backing that had not still existed in her era. Intrigued by his tact, she turned the portrait over, and saw the unmistakable handwriting, faded but so very dear.

Christy,
I'm safe I♥U
KitKat 1816

He watched her glorious face transform into that of a mad, glorious virago and thought ruefully, not for the first time, of the joys and heartaches this woman would bring him.

"She's here, at your house? You have her and haven't let me see her?" Her shrill voice reverberating off the darkened walls and he held a staying hand.

"No, I don't have her. She is not mine to keep or yet mine to share."

"You had better start explaining now before I scream and wake everyone in this house looking for her."

"She isn't here. That's the truth. And while you do not know enough to believe me, I can tell you she is perfectly safe." He pointed to the portrait she now held in a determined grip.

"Then where is she and why haven't you taken me to her?"

"Because as I said, she is not mine to…"

"I am going to count to three and then I will scream for help. One…" She faced him fully and squared her pert little chin. "Two…" He could see this exchange was not going to end well if she did scream down the house.

"Miss Ragland, stop. If you scream and wake the household, they will not help you. If you make a scene, I will not help you. Do … you…understand?"

"Ahhhh…no. Why won't you tell me where she is?"

"Because Miss Ragland, it is not up to me. I suggest you retire for the night. We…we will speak of this again in the morning."

"Oh, you bet your, your…butt we will speak of this again in the morning." She stalked to the door and slammed it for effect he was sure.

He hoped it made her feel better because she had certainly achieved her goal if it was to increase his already throbbing head.

"Beth, can I ask you straight up?" The maid had answered her call but stared at her warily. Well, she should be nervous, Christine thought, and plowed ahead.

Beth interrupted just as she opened her mouth. "Straight up? Ma'am?"

"You know, it's…how do I say that? Can I ask you anything and you will answer?"

"I will be honest, ma'am. I will answer what I can." But she also took a step backward. Beth's reticence for a serious question had Christine's instincts humming. She knew something.

"Fair enough." With that Christine took a deep breath. "Is my sister here, somewhere close by? I've seen the portrait and I can feel her."

"Ma'am, she is."

She wondered why Beth had not hesitated after all the other hedging but was next assailed by the realization she had found Kathryn. She had found her sister! On the heels of that revelation...

"Why am I being kept from her then?"

"Because they are afraid you will want to take her away and she is the Duke's now."

"Michael Stafford...that Duke? She is his? What does that mean, exactly?" Although she was fairly certain she knew exactly what that meant.

"He is her husband."

"She married a Duke? Willingly?"

"Yes. And by all accounts they are besotted with each other. There's a child on the way."

"A child?" Christine plopped onto her bed...a baby, a niece, a nephew, her beloved Kathryn's child? She was shocked and... overjoyed. Yes, that was certainly joy she felt, mixed with frustration over difficult males and why they were stonewalling her.

"Yes, she is with child and having a terrible time of it. The Duke has been frantic over her health. I think it's why he is so afraid of you."

"He is afraid of me?"

"Yes, he is afraid you will try to take here away."

"He's not holding her against her will, is he?"

"Oh no, she is quite happy with him although I daresay she misses you something awful." Beth hesitated. "She talks about you, about finding you."

"Then why is he afraid I'll take her away?"

"Unnatural fear if you ask me Miss. Can't figure out where you'd take her. She's his and that's just the law." She hesitated. "You aren't going to take her away, are you?"

Christine couldn't answer that question. She knew if they were married it would be unlikely Kathryn would leave her husband—her baby's father but... "Has she tried to leave?"

"Story is when she first came, she did...try to leave that is. To get home to wherever she came from and to you. But it came clear to all who saw them they were for each other. She made the vows to him but as I hear from my sister Ellie, has not one day stopped thinking of how to get to you."

4

ake up. Miss Ragland, Christine, wake up!" She heard
the pounding on the door through the fog of half-
sleep. She had lain awake until dragged into the depths by
exhaustion.

"Christine Ragland, I'm coming in!" And Matthew did with a
resounding smash of the door. "Get up now!"

She moved quickly, grabbing the pants she had stashed close by,
and dragging on riding boots that had recently magically appeared
in her wardrobe. He was pulling her out the door while her feet were
still stomping into them. He practically lifted her off her feet as they
flew down the stairs.

"I'm coming but tell me what's wrong. Where's the fire?"

"The barn!"

"Oh, I... Wait, that was just an expression. The barn...it's on fire?
Your horse!"

"Exactly. He's out as are the others. But, we've sent Thrasher to
ask Asterleigh for reinforcements. We need to keep the fire from
catching trees or grass. And if we can save the fencing..." He trailed

off as they rounded the corner of the house. Orange and red flames shot sparks high in to the air. Two hands were working a pump and Mrs. Soggs and Hunter were soaking rags, one of which Matthew promptly dropped onto her head.

"We're forming a bucket line. To keep the blaze from spreading." He yelled over the roar of flaming timbers. "The barn is probably... not salvageable, but we will try. I need you to keep watch for the cavalry and then get Knight to safety when Thrasher returns. And stay clear of the blessed flames!"

She opened her mouth. He was sure to argue, as the pounding of hooves sounded from behind her. She turned as the troop from Hawthorne thundered over the rise. Matthew felt a measure of relief as his oldest friend threw himself from the saddle and ordered his men into action. The trees, the house would be safe with this number of hands. But the barn...

Untold hours later, the flames had all but died and Matthew looked around but didn't see Christine. The acrid fumes rising from the sorry pile that had been his barn chased all but the final stalwart few out into fresher air. The sun was just peeking over the horizon. Where was Christine?

"I doubt her orders were to tote buckets," a sardonic voice came from behind him. Matthew stopped and angled his gaze toward Michael.

"As you say. I am sure I do not wish to know how she endangered herself," he admitted. "But I assume by your calm she is unharmed?"

"Oh yes, she is in fine fettle now. Come. I will take you to her." Michael started off toward the northernmost section of the property, bordering Hawthorne, where the terribly dirty American girl was overseeing two of Michael's stable lads and Hunter in keeping order among the large group of horses his men had ridden.

"Miss Ragland, I see you have honored my request to tend horses and steer clear of the fire." He knew she flushed although the soot marring her lovely face and the half-light of dawn did not give him the pleasure of seeing it."

"I am tending to horses. These are beauties...and these young gentlemen are helping me. Right guys?"

The lads, besotted as he expected any and all who came under the power of her presence surely were, smiled and bobbed. "His Grace asked us to help the lady keep the horses away from the fire," said one. "She's a right dab hand."

"That she is, lads. I will stay with the lady while you report to his Grace for your next orders. We can manage for a few minutes." He stepped closer to her as all of the boys clattered off in Michael's wake. He was sure he heard a chuckle. Turning to his guest, he touched her smudged cheek. "You did not completely avoid the flames, did you Christine?"

"No. I thought...well...I had an idea..." Her words trailed off as she looked in to his eyes. She would see concern, and fatigue but she would also see the desire he could no longer keep at bay. This small, fragile woman had battled flames and at the same time managed to organize a makeshift corral for the horses. "At home, we have fire hoses. They are tubes that suck the water in. Almost like a canal, but that you can hold. I need more time and materials to create a hose."

"Your idea is intriguing and I'm grateful for all you were willing... are willing to do. Now I must go and help get these beasts settled in Asterleigh's stables."

"I'm coming with you." If he had thought she would let him go without taking her, he should have known she was no longer going to be denied the reunion with her sister.

"Yes."

"Yes? Just like that? No argument! What? No longer afraid I will abscond with Kathryn?

"No. I know you will not." And he turned away before she could see the question in his eyes.

Christine's lids drooped, and her hands dropped. The grip of her knees wobbled. But physical exhaustion could not diminish the intense joy building inside her. More than four months had passed since she had seen, talked to, laughed with, or hugged her favorite person in all the world. Nights awake, fear keeping her from sleep, paralytic anguish at the thought of Kathryn kidnapped or murdered, were ending in moments. She would not truly believe Kathryn was safe until she saw her, but with every step on the gentle mare she was riding, the dream was coming clearer.

Not prepared for the grandeur of Hawthorne, Christine blinked as the Duke's home rose out of the dawn mists like a storybook castle with flags flying and lights blazing. She took in the old stone parapets and fantastic windows just as the main doors were flung open.

Her troop clattered to a stamping halt just as a diminutive figure appeared in the opening. Draped in flowing robes with burnished hair spilling down her back, Kathryn Ragland Stafford took the first step down the short stairs and froze. The jolt of recognition hit Christine and she watched her sister's eyes turn from concerned joy at seeing her husband to puzzled to shocked. She started forward and her movements shook Christine into action.

Christine flung herself to the ground in a controlled crouch and took off running. Kathryn, too, aimed for her and the crowd of milling horses and tired men parted like the Red Sea. She felt the impact. It knocked her back when Kathryn flung both arms around her. They would have fallen to the ground had the Duke not scooped both of them into his massive arms and begun walking toward the open doors.

"Christy! I ...you...you're here." Kathryn pushed from the Duke's arms as they reached the threshold and stopped the entire procession.

Christine watched her elder sister choose her words carefully and was utterly gratified that soon, the people who had kept them apart would be getting their ears filled. "There's quite a story I imagine going on here, but we have an audience, and everyone is clearly exhausted, and dirty," said the sister who looked very much like a duchess. She was stunned most of the males scattered and ran at her sister's command. Only the two whom she knew were due for the earful stayed. Even they shifted in their boots.

"Hallthorpe! Will you show Miss Ragland to..." she said with what Christine could see was relish and emphasis. The stately butler's eyes actually bulged as she added, "...her room to freshen up. Maybe Ellie can be called to assist her?"

Christine did not mistake the tone and she was sure the audience of gentlemen did not either. She was surprised they had not scrammed with the others. "Oh, and I imagine she and Beth can first join me in my chamber for a moment." Her sister's slow, silky, almost scathingly correct diction boded as poorly for the hapless maids. Well, they had been under orders to be deceitful, hadn't they?

Then she turned the full weight of her small but lethal smile on the Duke. Christine almost giggled—almost. "And then we will join you in your study. Say half an hour?"

"As you say, Your Grace." And finally, all of the remaining men beat a hasty retreat.

This room was as different from the one she had been assigned in Matthew's house as it was from hers at home. Almost. The wealth on display was mindboggling. Had she ever seen silk bedding piled so high in such a dramatically feminine bed? Had she seen windows so tall and draped with sheening curtains tied back with golden ropes? Or a full set of what had to be genuine silver combs, brushes, and cream pots.

The scrape had her turning back toward the door. A uniformed maid stood near the opening eyeing her as warily as Christine supposed she was. Was this the famous or infamous Ellie? The sister of the maid who had been serving her at Worley? "Her Grace wanted you to know she's detained in the study for a few minutes but hopes you will make yourself at home."

At home? Here? "It's a lovely room."

"She thought of you when she had it done, Miss."

"She, you mean Kathryn? Sorry, the Duchess, did this for me?" She turned a full circle this time and took in the colors. The old golds and greens in every shade were exactly the tones she would choose if she were doing the room herself.

The maid had been wary but seemed to stiffen her spine. Christine could hardly look less threatening, covered in soot, her hair gunked with ash. Talking as she walked fully into the room toward Christine, Ellie pushed her down onto the lovely and too clean stool in front of the mirror. "We can get you cleaned up before Her Grace gets through telling His Grace what she thinks of this latest start of his and then you and she can have a nice coze."

"I caught a look at myself. I think it's going to take a lot more than just a brush to make me presentable."

"Don't you worry, we've had time to get ready."

While Ellie pulled the brush through her knotted hair, Christine worked the buttons of the damaged shirt. Her riding pants, too, were probably beyond repair. As she wondered what outfit they were going to produce for her this time Beth came through another door and opened a large armoire Christine had not yet peeped into. Hanging there were several gowns, in the same colors as the fabrics of the room. Christine had not imagined her sister had actually prepared a room, and clothes, and she now suspected every comfort, for her. "This is all for me? She did this?"

"She did. She said as how if she couldn't look for you, she could prepare, and she could pray. And here you are." Brisk, businesslike now, Ellie had her hair untangled and proceeded to produce a complicated braid. Beth had chosen a gown of green remarkably like her eyes and a footman she had not before noticed was slipping out with empty buckets.

When Ellie stepped back, presumably to judge her creation, Beth stepped in with a wet cloth. The first touch of the warm water relaxed Christine as Beth gently scrubbed her cheeks, forehead, and dirty neck. The shirt came carefully over her hairdo and Beth began to clean her fingers. Had she ever been so completely spoiled? She remembered Kathryn braiding her hair and painting her nails during late night beauty sessions. The pang came swiftly and sharply...the lost months, the dramatic changes.

She knew Kathryn was pregnant. Had she been able to tell? The night gown and robe flowed and billowed but there had been something in the way she stood. As they hugged, there was not the stick thin sister she remembered. Oh my, Kathryn was going to be a mom. She would have a baby niece or nephew to spoil.

On the heels of that joyous revelation was the other one. The only way she would be here to spoil that niece or nephew was if she stayed...in the 19th century. Could she? Kathryn had...

"There you are! Look at my incredibly beautiful, slightly dirty, fabulous baby sister." Kathryn grabbed her tightly and held on. Christine squeezed but just as quickly wondered "...the baby? Is it okay to..."

"Don't worry. Hugs are perfectly fine. So those scoundrels told you that, did they?"

"No, I think it was Beth, once I cornered her? I'm not sure who said it first, but it was not your husband or his equally tight-lipped friend."

"Oh, don't worry, those two are in for a good bit more from me, but I decided to stop and let them have a minute to recover while I came to see you. Let me look."

The maids had stepped back to let Kathryn hug her but once again Ellie stiffened her spine and came close holding the lovely gown. "Oh yes, that one's perfect." Ellie slipped the gown over her head and Kathryn began pulling the laces tight. "I don't know where to start. I want it all, every bit. How you got here? What is happening in my absence? How they kept you from me?

"I can start with that last one. Those men downstairs were afraid —and specifically your very large horse-riding, fire-fighting husband —that I would steal you away. I believe he had to be sure I wasn't a threat to him before he was going to let us meet."

Kathryn snorted. "He sort of got overridden by the fire."

"Yes, that's a problem too. I am sure we will talk about it, after we talk about your arrival and what else they have avoided telling me."

"I'm not sure there's a lot you're missing other than the how. I'm assuming my trip was something like yours...the paintings in the set, right?"

"I thought that might be it." She grabbed Christine's shoulders and squeezed triumphantly. "I guess you found my note? I thought Matthew, or someone would have the others in this time period. Dang, I'm good."

"That you are big sister. But your note did not survive into the 21st century. It was a good try though. Now, let's go tell some arrogant Englishmen what's what." They linked arms and headed toward the door and down to beard the lions.

She heard the rumble of male voices. They were talking low,

conspiratorially, but she suspected they stopped as soon as they heard the pat of lady's slippers in the hall. Best they should stop plotting anymore. She was ready to give them a piece of her mind. And get an apology, and some more explanations.

"Gentlemen?" Her sister, now very much the Duchess again, sailed into what was obviously her husband's study. The men were standing. Her former host bowed over her sister's hand. The Duke reached for it too, but his wife evaded him. Christine knew she was not happy with either of them.

The Duke, Michael Stafford, her newly found brother-in law, waved her to a sumptuous chair nearest the fire and close to his own desk chair. "Miss Ragland, welcome to our home."

"Thank you, Your Grace...Michael." She saw the twinkle in his attractive and quite warm brown eyes. "It's lovely isn't really the right word."

"No, sister, you're right. Hawthorne is magnificent!" Christine heard the sharp edge in Kathryn's voice and shot her a brief quelling look. *Let me try this first. My battle, this time big sis.*

"I haven't figured out exactly where to start but I know one thing, Michael, I'm angry with you. And you, too." It was easy enough to shoot a glare Matthew's way just because he deserved one too.

"I know..." Michael started to speak but she interrupted the Duke with an upraised hand.

"I'm sorry, but I'm going to say this. You had no right. No right to keep us apart, to decide for us we couldn't be trusted, or whatever nonsense you thought." She took a breath but had no intention of letting him off the hook.

Although she was just getting started, she did not mistake the low and lethal voice getting her pronouncement. "Miss Ragland, you are mistaken. When it comes to Kathryn, my wife, I have every right."

She sighed. "You really think I was going to steal her away?"

"I will accept your tone and your contempt, but only in this. I did not know how you had gotten here. Kathryn herself does not really know how she got here. I was not going to risk a reverse of the amazing circumstance that brought her to me and have her vanish with you."

She watched him and saw the warm intensity in his eyes as they rested on Kat, the focus, and the power of that gaze. He was a man clearly in love with her sister. And he was genuinely afraid of the unknown force that had brought her to him. Christine knew she was staring. She had not ever seen that kind of devotion. Her brother-in-law's sincerity inspired her to choose her next words carefully.

"I think I understand. Neither of us is sure of the how. We know about the paintings. You know that too, right?" All of them nodded.

"Yes, we are aware they have some role. Go on," Michael said.

"But that's it. I don't really know how I got here but I know my heart was looking and I found. I'm still a little mad at both of you, but I guess I can understand your fears. It's hard to fight your reasoning or your obvious...love for Kathryn." The Duke's lashes swept to his cheeks. "I was beside myself for every minute she was missing."

He reached for her hand and gestured for Kat. Her sister slipped onto his lap, laid her head on her husband's broad shoulder and they squeezed hands forming a triangle.

The tears came. Christine couldn't stop them. And then there was a handkerchief and another hand, this time on her own shoulder. And they sat in that frozen tableau of joy and disbelief until her tears ran dry.

rother, I heard a wonderful rumor...Oh, look...." The slender brunette lady who had barged right in to the room turned her radiant smile on Christine and reached out both slim-fingered hands. "You must be Christine. I heard you had found your way to us. Kathryn must be ecstatic."

"She was quite overjoyed as you say, my dear. She hasn't yet risen this morning, however." The Duke and the lovely lady were both staring at her and she was still held in the lady's hands. No one had introduced them or really even given her a chance to answer.

"I'm sorry. You don't know me. I'm Cassandra...the sister of this autocrat. I understand you've had occasion to meet him...prior to being reunited with your own sister." The raised-brow look Cassandra bestowed on her brother was better than any rejoinder Christine had come up with herself so she chose to let the words stand. "Tell me how you find our...how shall I say it, hospitality?"

"I've been treated like a Princess if that's what you mean?" She had a strong feeling Cassandra was referring to the Duke's arrogant dictates about who will see who when and she had no doubt Cassandra knew where she stood on being dictated to.

"Michael, I wanted to talk with you and Kathryn about the wedding. I know the timing, with what happened last night is terrible...but...I...need..."

"My dear, we are capable of managing the wedding and, Lord Worley will be able to organize his plans at the same time. I do, however, have a proposition for you and your intended. Where is he this morning?"

"Jem rode over shortly after everyone arrived here to keep watch in the night. He knew whoever had remained behind must be tired. He thought he could help." She shrugged.

"I daresay, Matthew is grateful. But since your fiancé has gone to do exactly as I was going to ask, I will share with you our plans. We, Matthew and I, would like for you and Jem to move in to Worley. You can be chatelaine and even more importantly, Jem can be bailiff."

"Wait. You want Jem to run the farm?" She looked...shocked?

"I thought...I'm sorry, was I wrong?" he asked.

Christine saw once again the big strong soldier's eyes turn compassionate and unsure? "No, I mean... yes. I don't know what I mean...oh, Michael," Cassandra jumped into her brother's arms, knocking her chair back against the wall buffet. Serving dishes clattered bringing staff rushing in from three directions. The Butler named Hallthorpe, who Christine could see obviously had some telepathic way of communicating with the others, had the mess cleared away before Cassandra stopped exclaiming.

"I take it by this display you approve of our direction?" He lifted her chin and looked into the tear-stained face. Christine had seen compassion, care and love from this man and now was sure she understood why Kathryn had married him. Their own Father had thought always only of himself. This man obviously cared for his family and she felt profoundly happy to be able to approve of Kathryn's choice.

As if her revelation conjured Kathryn, her sister breezed into the room. "You're here. Wonderful. I wasn't sure you'd be down yet after such a long night. I should have realized..." Kathryn blushed slightly. Was it because of her pregnancy? She must be embarrassed to not be able to get out of bed after being up late herself. The unnerving thought that the big sister who had been invincible when they were growing up was not able to keep her usual schedule refused to lodge itself in Christine's head. Nothing, nothing was actually going to keep Kathryn down. Christine would make sure of it.

"Are you sure you're up to this darling?" Cassandra had asked Kathryn several times that morning during their conversations and Kathryn had calmly told her she was fine. Was she, Christine wondered? She saw dark circles and signs of fatigue on Kathryn's normally animated face.

"We've got three days, Cass, and everything is going to be perfect. Now tell me again what we decided about the way you are leaving." Her sister shifted the papers in her lap and Christine was able to study Kat's figure. She did have a very obvious baby bump and Christine noted with a jolt those several times Kathryn placed her hand on the baby.

She could still not quite believe all of the amazing things that had happened to both of them, but the advent of this child was the most awe inspiring. Kathryn was so loving and strong and smart. What a wonderful mother she would make. With that thought, another just as strong, as definite, struck. Christine would have to be here for the baby's birth, for the raising of him or her. She could not imagine otherwise. She was going to have to accept this life because she was not going to leave this time and place and leave Kathryn and her baby behind.

There was nothing to go back to anyway, was there? They had no family to speak of. She could do what she loved most here. Horses were a significant part of life in this century. Her expertise would be welcomed, wouldn't it? She could work with horses to her heart's content. And Kathryn clearly needed her. Not in any way to care for her physically, she had an overprotective husband and staff for that. But she needed someone like her, to be her friend and companion. To be the sisters they had always been.

"Where have you gone, Christy?" Kathryn was studying her through concerned eyes.

"Here actually. I was thinking about being here with you and your new family and the baby." She reached for her sister's hand.

"You can probably imagine how I have missed you. How I have been experiencing such profound joy," and she looked at Cassandra, and placed her free hand on her belly, "and such bitter grief all at the same time. No wonder Michael is worried about me. I've been a mess." She gave a watery laugh.

"Well, you'll be a mess no longer. I'm here." She squeezed. "I'm really here and I'm not leaving you." Her declaration was met with another burst of tears.

"I'm so grateful. I don't have any idea how our friends and colleagues are going to understand our disappearances but we're where we're supposed to be, I believe."

"Well, I for one concur with you both," Cassandra declared. "Now can we finalize that seating chart? I've got to finish packing!"

"May I cut in?" The man was smooth, and gorgeous! Christine knew she was staring. He had the exotic good looks of a fashion model and the slight accent of France. Then he chuckled. "I can see on your lovely face, you have not heard of me. Weatherford...for my sins."

She knew she still looked confused and she felt the warmth spread in her cheeks. She had been caught staring. How gauche, the country bumpkin at the society wedding. Well, not society exactly but it was a wedding in a Duke's ballroom. "I'm sorry, I haven't really met many people. Lord Weatherford?"

"His Grace, the Duke, had been remiss in introducing you around. But the rumors of your beauty are not exaggerated." She pinkened again at the idea she was rumored to be anything, but she knew the Duke had spoken about her and her sister with his friends. Presumably, at this small, select gathering, this gentleman was one privy to her personal information. "I see I have distressed you. I am so enjoying our dance, don't let your discovery of Asterleigh's high handed-ness spoil it." He chuckled. The jerk.

"I can't help it. He knows so much about me, and then he kept us apart..." She trailed off. This man may know about her, but he didn't need to know all that!

"My dear, if you ever play cards, you will need to wear a mask covering those lovely green eyes of yours. But alas, I am one of Asterleigh's closest friends. I know about your situation, and your sister's." She followed his gaze to where Kathryn and the Duke were still greeting guests at the double doors. "In fact, I was one of the first people she met, when she was attempting to escape"

"Oh, you're the one who picked her up in the woods. She told me about you. She was right. You are dangerous."

"Not to you my dear, not to you." She thought he'd be dangerous to anyone, but she felt the touch on her elbow and her heart leaped. And she realized why he was smiling knowingly.

"Julian, you are not corrupting our lovely visitor against us lesser mortals, are you?"

"Ah, see, I've been found out..."

Matthew laughed, and deftly swung her into his arms, away from his friend, and smoothly back into the turns of the dance. She thought it might be a waltz. She really didn't know the steps, but he practically carried her across the floor anyway. It felt completely natural to put her slippers onto the toes of his boots and let him control their movements.

They didn't speak but she watched his handsome face and savored the small and fascinating laugh lines around his eyes. He probably spent time in the sun without a hat. She wanted badly to trace them. To finger the strands of the severe cut of his hair which showed even more the wide, strong brow and a small scar at his temple. Matthew Drake made her inexperienced nerves jangle.

"Miss Ragland, I hope you are enjoying yourself." He smiled into her eyes.

She gulped. "I am. Yes, it's...lovely. I've never...been to a ball before."

"If I might be permitted, you fit naturally as if you had been born to it."

"It helps that you're doing all the work. I don't actually know how to do any of these dances."

"Ha, it is fortunate no one can see us. I daresay a matron or two would be scandalized."

"I've heard that. Good thing we didn't have time to hem this dress."

When she laughed, her entire face lit up. He could not explain how her smile made her even more achingly beautiful. She was simply the most exquisite creature he had ever seen, and he needed to stop ogling her. "You are settling in...at Hawthorne?"

"Oh, do you really ever settle in at a Duke's castle? I mean, I have a gorgeous room, servants, unlimited meals prepared for me, people to dress me..." He raised an eyebrow and looked around.

"Oops, was I not supposed to say that?"

"Not if anyone else can hear. But I am not offended."

"Good because I'm not used to every other word I say being off limits. Yesterday, I asked Kathryn how she was feeling at breakfast and the Duke looked at me like I had said a bad word."

"Michael? He was probably more interested in the response than the inappropriateness of the question. His bride I believe does not want him worrying so she isn't completely..."

"Honest?"

"I was going to say forthcoming. But no, she probably doesn't tell him the truth about her health."

"Women have been getting pregnant and working through it since the beginning of time. You would think men would get used to it. Instead, you all get so nervous and overprotective."

"I will admit, I've never seen him so concerned. And this is another of those subjects the tabbies would disapprove."

"Well, we're whispering."

"Since we are going to break all the rules, let me ask you about your...vocational plans." He hesitated. "Well, I was hoping... Hmmm, I can't seem to come up with the right word. I do not believe it is proposition."

"Are you looking for the word offer?"

"I believe so but that too is really probably not correct. I was wondering, since you have skills I will need but no credentials to practice your craft in the wider community, if you will assist me with my breeding program."

"I wasn't expecting to be able to practice. My license, even if it had magically transported over with me, wouldn't do me much good. I don't think Auburn has been founded yet." His relief was profound. He had feared she would be stubborn, as her elder sister had been, about returning to her home. This sister seemed to have accepted her place here. But he was not above probing further. He, like Michael with his find, was not letting her go. "I have a horse I would like you to work with. She is a filly from your sister's horse, Jasmine."

"Oh, are you talking about the gorgeous mahogany thoroughbred with the patterned forehead? She's yours?" He loved the way her eyes lit up when she talked about his horses.

"She is, but how I got her is another inappropriate story."

"Oh, you have to tell me, please!"

"I shall do that, but this dance is ended. Will you walk in the garden with me and I will tell you how the beautiful, dainty English lady horse met the big Welsh thoroughbred racer."

He had wanted to prolong their time together. He had not seen enough of her since she moved in with Asterleigh and his bride. The rebuilding of the barn preoccupied him to the exclusion of all else and the wedding plans kept the ladies indoors tied to their lists. No doubt the continuing fatigue of Her Grace had contributed as well. He knew Christine had been helping Cassandra with final wedding preparations and he had it on good authority Christine had been visiting tenants in her sister's stead.

He also thought he knew, or hoped he was right, that this sister had accepted her lot. He truly believed she was not attempting to leave and she was certainly expressing her determination to be by her sister's side when the child was born. His greater fear, much as Michael's was, was that the wonderful happenstance that had brought her here would work in reverse and send her home.

He had not doubted she was exactly as she said, from another time and place. He simply wanted to keep her in his. She fit. Her intelligence helped her adapt and her skills were ideal. Who would have known the woman who almost quite literally fell out of the sky into his lap would be trained to care for animals? It was as if she had been made just for him.

"You look awfully serious. I thought you were about to tell me a story unfit for public consumption."

Was he that transparent? Wiping the chagrinned expression from his face, he threaded her hand though the crook of his arm and headed for the section of the garden farthest from the sounds of the ballroom. "The story is not fit for the tabbies' ears because it has all manner of inappropriate activities. I am not sure I can tell you without blushing."

"Well, if I'm going to help you with your breeding program, you are going to have to get used to talking frankly with me. I don't think I could take an entire conversation about breeding, conception, gestation and birthing with veiled references to delicate conditions, her time and what is that other one...indisposition?"

"Just so, Miss Ragland." With her he laughed. It felt so good to laugh again, and he knew it was the incredible creature on his arm who lightened his mood from the worry and dread plaguing him these last days. For a few minutes he would allow himself to forget his problems in her company.

And as he was becoming accustomed, she interrupted his musings. "Oh, I think you should call me Christine or Christy when we are talking inappropriately. Surely this is a time we can be informal. And I will know we're about to whisper."

"Alright, then you should call me Matthew." The chuckle escaped, wonderfully!

"Do you mind if I tell you Matthew sounds too formal for secret conspiratorial whispering? Do you have a nickname?"

"My brother called me Matti, although that doesn't seem to fit this situation either. We were very young." He sighed at one more sad memory.

"What about Matt? You call me Christy and I will call you Matt. Then we will whisper and say what we need to about the horses. And if we whisper into our fans or hankies, all the ladies watching will think we are talking about your lovely English weather."

"And then you will tilt your head, give one perfectly restrained giggle, and I will bow over your hand. We will look remarkably respectable."

"Now, about that story."

She lay in bed recalling the lovely cadence of Matthew's voice as he told her the raucous tale of drunken lords, loose stable locks, an amorous horse and a willing filly. And as she thought more about him, he didn't actually seem like a Matt after all. He was Matthew with that way he had of bringing to life such a scandalous and funny story in his own understated, dignified manner.

He was like no other man she had ever met, strong and courageous, but also gentlemanly and even gentle. She was deeply afraid she was falling in love with him.

The morning light did nothing to dispel the disturbing realization she was bound to him like she had been to no other man. Why she was so afraid of her feelings she did not know. Had she not already said she was staying? Why could she also not have feelings for someone in this dimension? Was it because she had never found anyone to care for before? Was it her inexperience causing this barrier to trusting a man? As if her thoughts conjured the one person most likely to understand her fears, Kathryn appeared on the path heading for her and her stone bench perch. "How did you find me?"

"You think so loudly. I can almost hear all of those troubles calling to me. What's wrong, Christy?" Her sister patted her knee affectionately and relaxed onto the bench beside her, draping the warm shawl around her shoulders. She had not allowed for the cold air.

"You know me so well. You can't imagine how..." She sighed. "Of course, you can. Sorry."

"Yes, I can imagine how awful it was for you all those weeks. Only, I had Michael and so many new and wonderful feelings to jumble in alongside the awful ones. I was constantly wondering what was what. Tell me, baby."

Leaning her head against the shoulder that had always been her favorite was like another form of coming home. "I'm interested, is that the word here, in Matthew Drake. And that is so different for me. No one has ever even been enough of an interest to bother with. Well at least no human had been interesting enough. Now, I've got that jumble you were talking about."

"The jumble is good when it's just about exploring new feelings."

Christine reached for her sister's hand. "I've seen the way he looks at you. He can't stop. No matter where you are in the room, his eyes are tracking you."

"I think I felt that. You should have seen how quickly he cut in on me dancing with the gorgeous and sexy Lord Weatherford."

"Oh, I did, and you are so right. Matthew made a beeline for you. And Julian is incredibly beautiful. I have no doubt Michael wasn't pleased it was Julian who found me during my escape attempt and then spent several hours alone with me in bringing me back."

"What's his story? How does anyone get that handsome?"

"He's half-French. They say his mother was so beautiful his father was dazzled. He clearly won the gene lottery. And, he's an only son and heir to an Earldom. So, with his looks and fortune, the women practically lay at his feet." She chuckled, and Christine realized she felt better. Not only because Kathryn had successfully changed the subject from her troubled thoughts but also because she had somehow made her actually feel sorry for a handsome, rich guy. That was the talent of Kathryn Ragland Stafford—women's counselor, raving beauty, new Duchess, star big sister.

6

I am not pleased to see so many hands rebuilding the barn. There are Asterleigh staff working with the ragtag band of holdovers we were not able to chase away from Worley. I believe it is time for another move." The malevolent gaze turned from watching his target's farm to plot his next move.

Miles away, blissfully unaware of the evil plans taking shape against Worley, Christine prepared for her first day of work. Of course, she knew caring for the horses would only be allowed so far. She could not be seen doing what would be considered actual work. She could reasonably curry her own horse, the one she had been loaned, and ride her, feed her or consult on her care, but she could not be seen to be managing the barn or directing activities. Fortunately for the men involved she was not, nor had ever been, someone who had to be obvious.

She could, and would, be perfectly comfortable nonchalantly

studying the horses without taking actions to raise eyebrows. She did not see this as cowering to male sentiment. She simply understood she was not at home and was perfectly willing to act in a ladylike manner. No one had to know once she was alone in the barn...well that was another matter altogether.

Jasmine was clearly thrilled to be saddled. Since Christine understood no one actually rode her sister's horse in her stead, she could only imagine these last weeks of frolicking in the pasture either alone or with other horses was not enough real exercise for a horse of Jasmine's quality. She understood the horse's excitement, not having seen the fascinating Matthew Drake for far too long for her own mind as well. The filly that ranged beside them however, was not as happy to be tied to her dam. Fleur Estreille danced and jigged her way to Worley making their trip half-again as long as it should have been.

The rhythmic sounds of hammering reached her ears and as the house came into sight, she could also see the very real shell of the new stable standing against the green of the distant hills.

Hunter came running to help her with the horses and she watched Matthew Drake push away from the fence where he lounged. He had been expecting her. She should not be reading anything in to his being attentive to her arrival. "Ain't she a beauty, Miss?"

"She is, yes. She's also frustrated with us and the slow pace. She needs the fidgets worked out." Christine was speaking as much to the man who joined them as to the boy who was jigging in his shoes to get his hands on the filly.

"Why don't you put her in the paddock," Matthew said to the boy "and we'll let everyone get a good look at her while she gets a run."

"She's going to get a lot of attention I can see." Christine's gaze had locked on the small group of very young men and boys perched on the railing admiring their newest guest.

"She's certainly beautiful but she's also important, to this stud and what we are going to do here. I think they've been as excited about her arrival as I have." He shot their audience a conspiratorial wink.

"I'm looking forward to hearing about your plans. I know you are talking about breeding...racers? Is that what has everyone so excited?"

"Well, it helped we had the opportunity to bring her here, and that she is of a line with a name in the sport."

She could imagine having a racing program would be both exciting and a tremendous amount of work. She knew it would be costly. How was he going to manage starting a thoroughbred breeding program being as near to broke as she was sure he was? But she also knew better than to ask him now and it was easy to notch up her smile and dive right in. "Show me the construction project. It is coming along remarkably in such a short time."

Matthew was expecting Michael and was working through his plan to distract Christine from their discussion of the information Michael was bringing. He greatly feared his friend had more bad news. The brief message asking for a meeting had been ominous. With the fire, and the debts, he was fast becoming worn to the bone.

"I hear you have a new hand." Matthew heard Michael from across the paddock and as he straightened, his new unpaid employee joined her brother-in-law at the fence. Not waiting for his answer Michael inquired of the horse. "How is she acting now that she's had the day with you?"

"Oh, she's mischievous. She hasn't let us saddle her yet. We gave up after she knocked down Hunter." Matthew had watched and wondered how Christine would handle the recalcitrant beast and decided she had treated the horse much as her sister had probably treated her. Fleur thought she won the round, but Christine Ragland was going to win the war.

"I've got those projections you asked me for. May we go into your study?" Matthew was sure Michael recognized the wisdom of avoiding the subject of his troubles in front of Christine. "And Christine, I am under orders to escort you home after our meeting. Will you be ready in an hour?"

"That will give me time to try to saddle her once more and then get her in for the night. Perfect. Jasmine and I will be ready."

They walked in silence toward the house. "Is she going to suspect?" Michael's mocking gleam told him the question was purely rhetorical.

"Oh, I wouldn't be surprised if she contrives an excuse to visit the necessary, then the kitchens or some such." At Michael's chuckle, he looked his question.

"As you are obviously wondering how I handle that intelligent, managing female I married, you know very well the answer is almost not at all. She has me at arm's length over her symptoms. I have to resort to bribing her maid, or most accurately, threatening her maid."

He opened the door himself for his guest as anyone who would normally do it for him was otherwise engaged in the construction project or any of the half-dozen other things his very small staff handled. Door opening was not one of them. If Michael took offense, he did not say as they walked side by side toward his private domain.

"How do you get away with that?" Matthew asked, genuinely hoping for the helpful wisdom.

"Ha, well, she only answers me when she knows it really wouldn't bother Kathryn for me to know," he answered ruefully.

"The women we have chosen are a trifle more work than some." At Michael's raised brow, he asked, "Did you doubt it? Now I've met someone not only beautiful and intelligent, she's also just right for the stud. I hope you approve because I would hate to have to damage our friendship over it."

"Of course. I want her safely and securely settled as close to Kathryn as possible. Your interest takes another burden away."

"I might be taking this one from your shoulders, but I never intended to immerse you in such a monstrous one as the troubles plaguing Worley. Tell me you have good news."

At Michael's dark look, Matthew's heart sank. Had he expected anything different?

"I do not have any good news, speculations only. I am beginning to think the players in this game are much more problematic than just the ones who we believe hold Seb's vouchers. Look at this letter from Hamilton."

Michael handed him the missive from their mutual colleague and childhood friend Colin Hamilton. Matthew read with a deeper sense of dread. "He says there's a connection to our former French friends, but he has information on Seb." Matthew continued to read. "Sebastian Drake was not as he seemed. What does he mean by that?"

"When I got Hamilton's letter, I sent word to Julian. He and I believe Sebastian had enemies not from the drink and cards crowd."

"Then who?"

"Bonaparte."

"How did Seb..." Matthew allowed his mind to travel back through his childhood. His memories of his big brother Sebastian were so clear, and so contrary to the ones illuminated by Sebastian's death. He taught Matthew to ride, and to swing a cavalry blade. Sebastian was the one all of the younger boys trailed, a bruising rider, good but not excellent student. Sebastian had been his hero. For him to fall so far, to turn to drink and gambling...his actions had never made sense, until now. "It wasn't real. He...he wasn't a wastrel, was he?"

"We don't believe so. Julian thinks it was likely he was hiding in plain sight, learning all he could in the hells. Maybe it all started as a lark. Help Mother England and all. That he developed debts would have had to be part of the game."

"But he did not mean to leave them unpaid? He planned to settle up after the war was over right and tight."

"Likely not. He probably got in over his head. Which also means he was doing something right. He probably was found out and silenced. That we all believed he died in a bar brawl over gambling debts tells me his enemy knew him very well and that we would believe the worst of him, and not look for deeper meanings."

"All of that makes sense about Sebastian. And I plan to spend a lot more time thinking about his being a hero rather than the other, but how do we get the connection between his spying endeavors to someone burning down my barn?"

"Here is where we don't have any strong evidence, just theories. Whoever knew of the spying wonders how much you know and is trying to keep you quiet."

"That doesn't make a lot of sense to me. I wasn't here. We hadn't run together since we were kids, certainly not since I had left for the continent."

"As I said, just theories. We should meet as soon as Hamilton returns. He could know a great deal more than he is telling."

"Summon me when you have him." As he and Michael rose to depart a commotion in the hall heralded the female whose presence he had expected much earlier. Today she would be disappointed. There was no more meeting for her to interrupt.

"Well, my dear, are you ready to depart?" Michael deftly turned his sister-in law toward the door, giving Matthew the time he needed to lock the desk drawer. It would not do for Christine to find that letter.

"I have a few instructions for Hunter. I'll only be a minute."

"Very well, I will meet you in the forecourt." He and Michael made for the door left open by Christine's invasion and he felt the gurgle of mirth in spite of the difficulties facing him.

"We were wrong. She didn't have enough excuses in her busy little head to figure out how to get in earlier."

"I have no doubt they will be plaguing me tonight. Kathryn has always been a handful but the two of them together, I cannot imagine."

"As you are besotted with your wife I will not take too much pity on you, friend."

"Ha, little you know. Just wait until you are married, and she is with child and you are worried and exasperated and...expectant all at the same time. You will no longer be laughing."

Matthew regarded his friend's departing back. Married...to Christine. Her with child. Those lovely visions went up in the proverbial smoke as he considered his dangerous enemy. If he wasn't killed or beggared or transported to debtor's prison, he could have her. Well, not before he laid the threat low.

"How are we going to learn what they are cooking up? You must have developed some spying techniques since you got here." Christine paced her sister's sitting room. Even though she was leaning against the lush pillows on her chaise clad in a loose peignoir, Kathryn's color was poor. She hadn't eaten enough at dinner. Christine had hoped that repairing to her sister's private domain and decrying autocratic men would put some color in her cheeks. When there was no answer from her normally insightful sister, Christine asked, "How far along are you?"

"Hmmm...fourteen, fifteen weeks I suppose. I'm not exactly sure. Why?"

"Aren't you supposed to start feeling better in your second trimester?"

"I...yes, I should be. Any day now. Rah rah." The question had done what the intrigue had not, gotten her sister's lively spirit back.

"I for one can't wait 'til you have a real baby bump. Right now, you still look perfectly slim but for the tiniest slope."

"You haven't been looking closely if you haven't noticed the other changes. My boobs are huge and sore, and I've probably gained five pounds around my middle."

"Considering you were a twig before, it's all for the good. But I guess you are showing a little." She plopped down next to Kathryn and laid her head gently on her sister's belly. "Can you hear anything? Does your husband listen?"

"He does exactly what you did. He leans in and kisses the baby. Then he tells me I'm beautiful and we end up in bed. It's wonderfully romantic."

"I'm so happy for you."

"But?"

"How did you know there was a 'but'? You always know the 'but' even when I try to hide it."

"You can never hide the 'but' from me. Can I guess?"

"You probably don't have to think too hard."

"No. I imagine you are wondering what I often did. How can I have such happiness knowing I will never go back?" She nodded her head against the baby while Kathryn continued. "I think maybe it's because this is where I'm supposed to be. I knew it at some point once I committed to Michael. My almost perfect life was only missing you. Now you're here it's completely perfect. There's nothing wrong, no reservations. I feel whole, in my heart, again."

"I'm happy for you. So happy you feel that way. I know there's really nothing back there, but it doesn't make it completely simple to accept. At some level I just can't believe this is my place."

"When it's right you'll know it. Oh, and I've got a few ideas about our sneaky guys now that I've gotten a bit of a rest in little sister!"

The daylight brought her a chance once again to work with the Worley horses. She was no less unnerved in the daylight, by her realization, Matthew Drake was her future but all the same, she knew spending the chill fall day in a warm stable surrounded by her favorite creatures would ground her like nothing else. She was also determined to put Kathryn's plan into place. It was quite genius to come right out and ask who they thought had burnt down the barn. Neither sister expected an answer, but it would give them a chance to hear what was said.

As her obsession came in to view she was rocked by another equally startling revelation. If something happened to him, what would she do? It would be like something out of a star-crossed lovers movie. She was agreeing to stay. She wanted him to be here with her. It would not be enough to be here with Kathryn and him not be part of her future, of her reality here. When she was within his line of sight, she tried to wipe her expression. She knew she wasn't as good as any of the Englishmen she had met at hiding her emotions but thought she had managed in time.

"Good morning, Christine."

"Matthew." He reached for her as she freed her booted feet from the stirrups.

"You'll see Hunter has managed to go for an entire day without a bump or bruise from our frisky filly." She laughed, she couldn't help it. And his boyish grin was intended, she was sure, to wipe her mind completely clean of arsonists and fire investigations.

"Is everything getting back to normal today?"

"If you mean, is everyone going about their business, I believe so."

"Actually, I probably should have just gone straight to the question I wanted to ask." And, she figured for good measure, she sent him the look that her big sister always used to win arguments before they started. "Have you learned anything about the fire?"

He checked. She saw he clearly wasn't expecting the direct attack.

What could he say? He had murderous, traitorous enemies lurking, waiting to kill him or anyone in their way. "I haven't learned who started the fire, no."

His non-answer said a lot, more she was sure than he had intended with that pause. He had learned something he didn't want her to know. "But you have ideas?"

"About who, no. But...possibly some of the why."

"Oh?"

"My brother had amassed debts. We don't know if any of his debtors may be trying to push the estate too far."

"You mean so you might be foreclosed on?"

"Something like that... It's a theory."

"You almost said 'it's one of the theories.' I could hear you hesitate."

"As you say." But he did not say anything further. They had reached the small knot of boys waiting to take Jasmine. "Do you have any specific instructions?"

He was clearly done with the discussion but as she waved Jasmine into Hunter's hands, she catalogued all she had learned. They did have theories—more than one including that someone wanted to steal the estate from Matthew. Or steal it in a way that looked legal—by collecting on gambling debts. That someone wanted to take Worley was probably true. Worley was a sprawling, gorgeous stretch of pasture-land bordering a Dukedom. Anyone would want it. As for the rest of his unsaid thoughts...well, she had somewhere to start.

The meeting had been arranged. Matthew paced his study to pass the time until he could ride for Hamilton. They had all agreed a meeting under Asterleigh's roof had too many possibilities for drawing the interest of unwanted spying female eyes and he was frankly tired of hosting his friends in his one decently appointed room with his poor selection of refreshments. He knew Hamilton certainly could provide a much-improved refreshment menu for the foursome.

While the ride would never previously have warranted a security escort, he determined he required support now with the malevolent forces seeking his demise. He had sent word to the stables for one of the hands to saddle a horse to join him. He worried even more about leaving Worley for any length of time, but he had to trust Jem's small but highly capable staff would be well-positioned to spot trouble. He would have to accept the precautions he had in place would ensure all would be well for a few hours.

He heard the tell-tale creak of leather and the clanking of stirrups as he stepped out into the fresh night air. Why was he not surprised to be greeted with twin jaunty salutes by two well-armed Asterleigh liveried grooms on horseback who had clearly charmed the youngster holding Knight's bridle. Matthew narrowed his eyes at the pair. At least one of the men looked vaguely familiar. "These gents said as how they'd see to riding with you, M'lord, if that be okay."

"Thank you, Franks. They will do. Find your bed, then. I know you have early chores."

"Thankee."

With these companions, Matthew could let the prancing horse have his head. Vaulting into the saddle, Matthew set his heels to Knight's side. On his nod, the three of them thundered out of the yard. The wind in his face, the chill air, the pounding, relentless pace freed him for this moment in time from the burdens of his situation. Riding was freedom.

As he passed the boundary of his land onto the corner of Julian's which snaked out and prevented his holdings from joining directly to Hamilton's, he thought of his half-French friend. How must it have been fighting against his Mother's countrymen? Surely it had been difficult to see those with his blood die, and to know he had a part in their deaths. He had never asked Julian.

He shook off those melancholy thoughts as he heard the distant barking of hounds. Colin's prized pack would be welcoming the others who were coming to the meeting from different directions. His riding companions, who had perfectly matched his paced across the miles, sensed his anticipation and spurred their horses in concert with his. The slight change in pace saved his life.

Matthew heard the crack and felt the whizz over his right shoulder. Knight surged, accustomed to the flight needed after such a sound. Matthew jerked his head toward the horseman cum guard on his right flank still riding fluidly low over his horse's neck. He checked his other companion and got an equally grim but certain brief acknowledgment. As they both seemed unharmed, there was no reason to stop to investigate and court further danger. So, the three of them thundered into the forecourt of Hamilton's comfortable country home at breakneck speed.

"I heard the shot. Are you alright?" Hamilton's normally jovial countenance was tight, worried, as he greeted them on the gravel drive.

"I'm fine. How about the two of you?" He nodded to the two guards who joined him at Colin's side. Jarvis, the man who had been on his left flank, slipped off his hat, a small nick in the brim.

"Well, this is a fine mess you've got, Matthew. Let's get inside." Colin's efficient groom hovered. "Haynes, will you take care of the horses so these men can get some refreshment?" The man led the horses away while Matthew's escorts headed for the kitchens and the beer he was sure would be waiting for them.

"I appreciate your looking out for me, friend. Apparently, I needed it." Matthew nodded ruefully at Michael's questioning stare and subsided into one of Colin's comfortable chairs in the very well-appointed masculine study.

"Was that a shot I heard then?" Michael asked.

"Just as the hounds started up. Convenient way to avoid detection. I didn't even try to tell the direction."

"No point. You were better off getting out of the woods. By the way, I am assuming my men are unharmed since no one is bustling about."

"Unharmed, yes. But you will be buying Jarvis a new riding hat." Michael's brows rose but neither spoke as Julian joined them, snapping the door shut with a resounding click.

"Gentlemen. I assume someone is responsible for the hole that will surely be found in one of my trees come morning?"

"If you find it, I will want to see. I didn't get a feel for where he was, only that we were about to cross over at the fork in the creek."

"One of my favorite spots. As boys, Colin and I would meet there at night when we were sneaking out."

"How come I never knew about that?" Matthew challenged Julian.

"Because we weren't altogether sure you wouldn't have told on us. Remember how righteous you were at eight?"

"A fine lot of good it did me considering I'm now facing debtor's prison or death at the hands of some unknown, possibly traitorous enemy."

"As to that," Colin spoke up. "I had word I shared with Asterleigh. Sorry, I didn't want to risk sending it to you in case the problem was in your household."

"No offense taken."

"You all heard the initial word I sent you. Sebastian Drake was not as he seemed. I believe in fact he was more than just an observer for the crown. Before I left, Manseri sought me out. Remember him?

"That Lieutenant loosely attached to Wellington? He knew about Julian, right?" Matthew remembered the part-Italian soldier who had

had some role in ferrying messages among their spymasters and Wellington.

"Yes, he was one of a very few who knew about Julian. Well, he also knew some about Seb," Colin added.

"I still cannot believe Seb had been working for the crown. He seemed such a wastrel those last few years." Michael shook his head.

"They believe he was onto an Englishman or French émigré turned spy. Our masters knew they were losing information that should not have gone away. They feared for Julian because several of the leaks were too close to his mission." Colin looked hard at Julian. "You, my friend, were found out, by someone. He wanted you dead. Manseri believes he yet lives and will still see you dead."

"I wondered about that brothel incident. Too pat, a fight in a brothel leading to the death of a soldier. I always thought that knife was meant for me."

"Yes, I believe your better taste saved you that night. I'm sorry for the young man but very grateful you survived."

"Well, now that we've reminded everyone of that nasty little piece of French trash, what does my pursuer have to do with what's happening now?" Julian asked Colin.

"Manseri and Jackman believe Seb had fingered the culprit."

"Wait, Manseri knew Jackman?" Michael started.

"Ah, none of us knew this but Manseri was Jackman's spy among spies," Colin announced satisfied he had everyone's undivided attention.

"I see it now. Someone targets my missions, kills at least one person in my place, takes untold pieces of information from my connections. They were letting me dangle as bait, weren't they? Watching for who came after me? And they had Sebastian watching from this side? He must have been tracking my informants. Was he actually watching my back too?"

"Manseri believes Seb would have blown his cover to save you if he had witnessed a direct order but he was always one step away.

Your nemesis was pulling strings and while he had a good idea who it was, he couldn't pin it down. One day he got too close."

"Matthew, I'm sorry. And...grateful." When Julian reached over and touched his shoulder, it was as if all the anger toward his brother, the grief over a seemingly wasted life melted away. His brother had been watching over his friend, had probably, most likely saved his life and given his own in the service of his country.

"Thank you. I'm desperately sorry he is gone but I'm glad you are alive my friend." And he meant it. Now he would not only have to find the killer, stop him before someone actually ended up dead, save his land from the creditors, and also begin clearing his big brother's name.

"Manseri gave me this." Julian took the paper from Colin, scanned the French and handed it to him. Matthew read the few words.

Who stands to gain the most if Julian Thornton dies without issue? The war is wonderful cover for murder.

Duforge? "Could the war be pretext for killing you? It certainly would have seemed that way. If your French uncle had learned of your occupation, he would have known many people in France he could have used to do his dirty work." Matthew saw the pieces falling into place.

"And their payment would have been information. That Julian carried. They wouldn't have needed money." Michael put that last piece of the puzzle together.

"So, the question is, how did your mother's uncle figure out what you were doing and who did he corrupt close to you?"

Julian had sat stoically during these last few minutes revelations. When he spoke, his voice was not recognizable. "She would have carved his heart out with a hairpin. Thank God, she will not know what he has done." Then Julian stood, fluidly. Even seething with anger his friend was fiendishly graceful.

"What do we know about him? Why is he targeting Worley

specifically now, other than the obvious—to keep Matthew from finding out what Sebastian did and what he knew?"

"He must believe I know of or have access to some of Seb's work."

"Or," Michael who had been quiet while Julian had seethed spoke up, "it's the proverbial two birds and one stone. He takes Worley away from Matthew to gain its secrets, but also to be adjacent to Weatherford. So he makes his case that as close family and the adjoining landowner he should inherit upon Julian's death."

7

$\mathcal{T}$here was a meeting last night," Kathryn announced as soon as Hallthorpe quit the room to refresh the teapot for the sisters.

"How do you know it was a meeting?"

"I'm such a light sleeper now that I have to go to the bathroom and shift all the pillows all through the night that I wake up at the smallest noise or movement. I waited 'til I heard the door and then watched him out the window. Michael thinks he's so smart walking the horses to the grass verge. But he can't even get his coat out of the closet without making some noise because while the others were spies, he was a soldier. And he's huge. He also had several men with him. No amount of stealth can keep all that horse rattling and clomping secret. Plus," she added with a laugh, "there was a note from Hamilton summoning them."

"How do you know that?" Christine exclaimed at Kathryn. Surely her sister's husband hadn't left the note where she could find it?

"I can see on your face what you're thinking. I didn't find it. I just know. I recognized the footman who delivered it and then I saw

Michael surreptitiously throw it in the fire. What else could it be but one of their 'men only' meetings?"

"Do we know what they talked about? Was it the possible 'theory' they've been pursuing?"

"Ah, the 'theory,'" Kathryn drew out the word. "I think there is a lot more going on than just someone collecting on Sebastian Drake's debts."

"Well, clearly big sis, you have some theories of your own. Spill them."

"We have to wait for... Oh, here she is now." Cassandra sailed into the room, color blooming on her cheeks.

"I'm sorry I'm late for the meeting I was..."

"Kissing your fiancé bye as he headed back to Worley?" said Kathryn. "We're not docking your pay for a little PDA, my dear.

"Oh, PDA, I remember that one. Kissing in public, right? Jem would be mortified if he knew you had caught us."

"Very well, you don't have to tell him. But now we've got to strategize. We don't have much time. Michael will return from his ride and he will start badgering me about doing too much."

"He seems to have chilled out a little since you started showing. Would you agree?" Christine said.

"Yes, I think he realized I feel better but I'm also not really able to do everything I would normally do anyway, so he doesn't have to watch me as closely. But baby talk later. Let's see what we know."

"We know Worley is in debt and the men are worried someone will haul Matthew off to jail. And we know someone may have tried to kill him," Christine catalogued to her co-conspirators.

"Kat's gaze whipped to hers. "What makes you say that? The fire was in the barn."

"Yes, but he fought it. And he might have fought it alone and died or died saving horses. Whoever is pulling these strings knows he would have rushed in to save the horses."

"And they would not have expected him to have summoned help so quickly from Hawthorne," added Cassandra.

"You're right, debtor's prison or death. Either one could see him lose Worley. So who wants Worley and why?" Kathryn looked from Cassandra to Christine.

"Why steal a horse farm? Is it the horses, the farm or... What is really valuable around here?"

"Hawthorne," both of her companions announced at once. "But," Kathryn continued, "when we ended the threat from Michael's cousin the direct actions here stopped."

"There is another valuable property adjacent to Worley," Cassandra said almost to herself as she spread marmalade on toast. Christine saw Kathryn's gaze sharpen. Hers did as well. "Maybe this is about Weatherford. It's valuable too and Julian has no Thornton family to speak of except that icky uncle on his mother's side. What's his name?"

"Duforge...is it Andre?" Kathryn touched her fingertip to her lip. "Yes, that makes perfect sense."

The loud male voice stopped all three ladies. They looked to the door just as the Duke strode through, windblown from his ride, a smile on his face for Kathryn. She could not deny that her sister's husband loved his wife. As he reached for Kathryn's hand, he tilted his head toward her and made Christine feel the weight of his regard for her sister.

Well, their conversation was effectively over with his arrival, but they had made tremendous progress. This business was surely about more than just Worley. It was about gaining a foothold in Herefordshire of several of the most prosperous properties, all under the guise of old debts or possibly even unsettled war business. She had much to pursue when she got to Worley today.

"Have you eaten, my dear?" Michael asked Kathryn.

"Yes, my love. I ate a little and drank some tea. I can't hold too much at a time, but I promise to have a snack in a little while." She only sounded a little peeved to Christine's mind, and likely just to poke the bear.

"That's fine. I have some business in my study." He turned to include Christine and Cassandra when he spoke again. "I know you haven't gotten out much lately, my dear, I thought you might like to ride in the cart with Christine today. We could tie the horses alongside and you could get some fresh air."

"You would let me ride in the cart? How did I manage that bit of luck?"

"I thought you'd like the fresh air and I have a selfish motive. I do not want Christine riding today. And before you ask," he held up his hand, "I will tell you why. There is someone out to do mischief and I'd rather you be in the bed of the cart if it comes than exposed on a horse."

"And you are going to let me go with her? I might faint." Her sister looked genuinely shocked. They were all surprised he would let Kathryn out of the house if he thought it was dangerous.

"The mischief doesn't seem to be during the day time. Once I told you what was afoot, you would insist, so I have arranged it as safely as I can short of locking you in your room until her return."

"That's more like the Duke I know." Kathryn fell into giggles and all of them joined her in laughing. If you couldn't laugh once in a while...

As she suspected, the group heading out in the winter chill for Worley was well-armed and escorted by two men who looked a lot more like soldiers than the local grooms or footmen she had seen around the castle.

She suspected the Duke had recruited some bodyguard talent. Christine didn't mind. She was looking forward to working with Fleur, getting some much-needed exercise, and seeing to Bleu's progress. The filly was nearing her time. Kathryn was draped in warm scarves relaxing against the pillows Michael had insisted she use, but nonetheless clearly enjoying being outside. Their guards were riding in interesting shifting patterns, most likely to be at the ready for attack.

She once again marveled at the twist of fate or the even more unbelievable shift in the time-space continuum that had brought her here just as her sister needed her, just as the plot to hurt Matthew had taken a decidedly nasty turn, and as the horses most certainly needed vet services. "Hunter."

The young man reached for her as she clambered over the side of the cart. "Lady Bleu sure is worrisome today, miss. She needs your attention, she does."

"Coming right away." Whatever she had intended to say in farewell to Kathryn was waved away.

"Go. Go. Me and my army will be fine." She waved a very Duchess-like hand to encompass the escort party. "But darling, I assume someone will be back to get you this evening."

"Tell me, what has she been doing?" Christine turned her attention, all-business on Hunter.

"She's been right anxious, miss. Pacing like they do." He trailed her into the stable.

"I'll check on her and then I want to hear about Fleur. No new bruises, I hope, for you, young man?"

"No, miss. She's been a lot better since we been riding her. Maybe just cause you came, she's happier."

"I can't take credit for her happiness, but I'm sure the regular exercise is doing her well."

As they entered the barn, she could hear the pregnant horse's restless pacing. "Me and Ben checked on her. She's blowing hard." Christine was certain they were just hours from the birth.

"Miss Ragland, are you in here?" Matthew said.

"Yes, but just coming out. You've heard what's been going on in here, I expect?"

"As you say, Hunter and Ben have kept me well-informed. I believe we are going to require some signals if we need to summon our resident doctor during the night."

"Where I come from, we would have beepers." She watched the frown beginning to form in his deep brown eyes so she hurried on, "But I'm sure a rider can reach me in plenty of time."

"I'm sorry." He shook his head and smiled at her. "I didn't mean to make you withdraw. I am not...afraid to discuss your origins."

She had seen the young men scurrying out the paddock door as Matthew had called to her so she knew they were alone. She reached for his gloved hand. "Thank you for understanding. I have that part of me. I can't un-know it. But don't worry, I'm not sorry I'm here. In fact, on the way over here I was thinking this is exactly where I should be. So many people need me. It feels good."

"And that is my cue to ask about your sister. I hear she was permitted to ride over with you."

"Can you believe he let her come? I figured it was because we were so well escorted, and that was the only possible reason. Did you notice our rather fierce looking escorts? "

"I did. I believe I recall one of them was an infantryman, probably one of Michael's sergeants."

"So ex-soldiers make good bodyguards?"

"As you say." She watched the small, self-deprecating smile form. She wanted to kiss him just there, on the fine lines fanning from his mouth. Instead, she touched him again, gently on the hand. He returned the caress, she thought understanding as she did, this was not the time or place for exploring their burgeoning feelings and motioned her to the open stable door.

Once she was out of his distracting presence, she could focus on what had transpired today, and through Michael's interesting revelations. None of the ladies would be fooled that they were not being hovered over and protected even more now with this obvious danger in the air, even if he had called it simply "mischief." What she was sure of was that the men had no clue how much of the danger, the life -threatening danger, the ladies had discerned.

The well-armed posse of guards had returned for Christine and borne her safely back to her sister's house. She learned that Kathryn was resting before dinner and was relieved the quiet would give her the opportunity to organize her medical supplies for the impending birth of Bleu's foal. She suspected the men had even planned how they would convey her to Matthew's if indeed the call to action came in the night. They had become quite obsessively protective. She was not offended by the concern.

If she had been at home, she would have also pulled out her favorite work jeans, the old pair of boots that had gotten her through many a weekend mucking stalls and a flannel shirt. Since none of those were going to be available for this birthing, she dug for the riding pants she had inveigled Beth to sew. The tails of the stolen man's shirt had been easy enough to tie off and the riding boots would just have to do for vet work. When Beth arrived to help her dress for dinner, Christine felt she was ready to take night call if needed.

"Miss, miss, they've sent a rider. You're to get up." Christine woke with a start at the insistent shaking by her maid. The night call had been only days in coming she realized. Beth was moving quickly toward the pile of clothes Christine had readied. They worked efficiently together to get her dressed and Christine was clattering down the stairs just minutes later.

She had forgotten to bind her hair and when she slid to a stop at the feet of her already-dressed and great-coated brother-in-law, she noticed the arrested look on his face.

"Christine, you are an amazingly stunning woman. Your hair is...exquisite."

The blush stung her cheeks, but she met his gaze. "Thank you, Your Grace, I'm told I resemble our mother."

"How fortuitous for us, then." He turned to look as the two guards emerged from the baize door at the back of the hall. He helped her into the riding jacket they had found for her that afternoon and gestured for her to precede him out the open door.

Four horses were saddled and waiting. "Oh, I forgot my bag." Just as she said it, Beth came hurrying toward them with her supplies. Her imperious brother-in-law reached for the bag and settled it on his pommel as one of the stable lads gave her a leg up onto her horse. She was last to mount and settle but within seconds, the four of them thundered out of the yard.

She didn't wait to be handed down but slid out of her saddle practically at the barn door, running toward the labored sounds. Michael followed more decorously with her bag. "Matthew, we're here," she called softly to him as she slid on the fresh hay at the open birthing stall door.

"She heard your voice." Matthew gave her a nervous smile. "I believe we are both quite glad you are here."

"Hello, darling, you are going to deliver a gorgeous baby," she crooned to the frightened horse as she ran her hands over the distended belly. "We will be here with you and at the end of it all you will be a mama. You will be terrific." The horse locked her terrified gaze with Christine's and seemed comforted by the words and the strokes of competent hands. "Matthew, I think she would like to rest her head in your lap. I'm going to see where we are."

"Are you trying to tell me to stay out of your way?"

"Only if you perceive it that way," she said giving him a brilliant smile of reassurance. "The sac is starting to emerge. I'm going to let her push a little on her own before I pull."

"I cannot believe how nervous I am now that I actually think of it." He shook his head and she saw the worry clouding his dark lovely eyes.

"Oh, Daddy, is this your first birth, as the owner I mean?"

"Yes, this is actually the first birth I have witnessed since well before the war. And of course there were stable hands and others to keep me from getting in the way."

She patted his hand and returned her attention to the mare. "There's a good push, just a little more and we will have the head." Christine marked the time as Bleu relaxed, panting onto Matthew's lap. When she tensed and blew again, Christine reached for the foreleg and tugged gently. As the laboring mare pushed, the foal's head slid free. She pulled the sac from the mouth and nostrils and touched the small nose. The tough little horse lifted its head. Since she could see its small chest rising and falling, she sat back and let Bleu relax.

Minutes passed as Bleu gathered her strength. When the horse once again blew and began pushing, Christine tugged gently on the forelegs. The baby's body slid free. She worked the sac off the legs and pulled first one and then a second hind leg free. She marveled at the midnight black colt pawing its forelegs at the now sticky straw. "Daddy, it's a boy!"

"A colt." His voice cracked. Matthew cleared his throat and worked to stand up himself. "Well, won't you look at him? He's stunning."

"He is and as hard as he's working to stand up, I can tell you'll have another little monster on your hands. Way to go, proud papa."

"And you, you were...magnificent."

"Bleu did all the work. I just made sure you didn't get in her way."

"You are too modest, Miss Ragland. We are quite fortunate to have you."

"My friend, I believe you're going to be the envy of our set." Both of them turned toward the new voice."

"Ah, Michael, isn't he..." As he choked, Christine turned to her brother-in-law.

"He is and so is our new doctor. We are indeed fortunate to have your expertise." He reached his arm to her, clearly intending to lead her from the stall and let Matthew enjoy his new foal for a few minutes alone. "I had been meaning to ask you about my wife."

She was intrigued. As they slipped out the stable doors into the quiet night, Michael wove her arm through his. "How exactly do you mean?"

"I'm quite sure you have been taking note of her color and how much she is eating? She looks better to me." She couldn't see his expression but heard the earnestness of his tone.

"Ah, yes, I agree. Since I first saw her, she's gotten her natural rosiness back. And I'd say she's gained a little weight." With her vision adjusted to the dark, she was able to watch his eyes as she said it and saw relief. "She needed to."

"I'm...grateful...for your arrival. And I know sharing this with me has put you in some difficulty as I know how stubborn my wife can be."

"Tell me something, Michael. What is it like...to feel that way? The way you do."

"It is at all times both joyous and frightening. For someone like me who is used to being..."

She finished his sentence, "...in command?"

"Ha yes. I would not trade it for my life. She, Kathryn and the life I have found with her, is...everything."

A second and a whoosh were the only warnings he had as Christine gasped and slumped against him.

"Worley!" The yell came from the garden gate.

Matthew's head whipped around at the sound and he saw Michael running toward him carrying a limp Christine in his arms. He sprinted toward the pair and what he saw terrified him, the spreading dark stain on the white shirt. "Arrow, from the woods. We need to get her to safety and stop the bleeding."

Matthew tripped up the short steps and burst into the hall, Michael with his bundle close behind him. "In here. On the chaise." His study being one of the few rooms fully furnished. *What next? Think!* "Soggs!" He yelled for his housekeeper. He needed supplies and he needed to see Christine breathing. Michael was arranging her on the low sofa on her side, an ugly arrow protruding from her shoulder, blood seeping slowly. "We need to stop the bleeding."

"And we need to know what's been damaged." Michael pressed his fingers on either side of the shaft while Matthew searched her chest for any sign the arrow had exited. He was both relieved and terrified the arrowhead was buried inside her.

"I want to get this out, but I don't know how much damage has been done."

"No. We need Bridelsby here before we remove it. Send a rider for him."

"Yes, right, I will." Matthew pulled away from the sheet-white form on the chaise only long enough to give instructions to Hunter who had followed his grandmother into the room, both hovering ready to help.

Soggs had assembled exactly what he would have asked for if he had been able to think properly. The sharp knife would do for sawing off the arrow. He could at least ease her discomfort while they waited by removing the long length of arrow that very likely did more damage with every bit of their jostling. He could only imagine the pain and very definitely focused on his task. Michael steadied Christine against his chest while Matthew worked at the wood. A low moan from the stricken form stilled both of them.

"Come now. We can do this. You can get that off," Michael reassured.

She said, "Ahhhhh."

"She's feeling this too much. Demmit," Matthew said.

"You've cut through enough it should break right in two." Michael gestured to the half-split shaft. "Go on, do it, one good break."

If Michael had not been here, would he have been able to manage? He needed to focus and get the arrow out so they could sit her upright and help her breathe more freely. He took one last pull of the knife through the wood where it gave on a satisfying snap. Her strangled gasp arrowed through him. Blessedly, her head slumped against Michael's bulk once more, the strained expression easing from her face. While he was grateful she had swooned, he was equally thankful he could see the rhythmic rising and falling of her chest. She was alive. She was here with him. And he was demmed sure she was staying alive.

"My lord?" Matthew's head snapped around at the sounds of the doctor and Michael entering the back parlor where he had taken momentary refuge after being dismissed from Christine's side by the pair. He stood on wobbly knees and took in their report while his ears rung, and his head spun. "We have the arrow head out. It knicked a bone and buried in muscle. I've got her stitched and she's sleeping. She'll be sore when she wakes."

"She's not bleeding any longer and has a little color," Michael reported.

It had been decided by someone that as her brother-in-law, propriety allowed he could assist the Doctor and Soggs in carrying her upstairs and sorting out her clothing.

"Thank..." Whatever he had been about to say was interrupted by a gaggle of female voices bearing down on them.

"Michael, how is she, where is she? What happened?" A red-headed dervish pelted them with questions as she barreled into the room.

"My love, calm down. I will answer all, but you must take a breath, relax, and calm down." Matthew watched in dazed amusement as Michael tried unsuccessfully to pull his tiny, agitated wife to the recently-vacated chaise. His gaze drawn in the direction Michael was pointing, he saw tell-tell signs of the recent occupant and decided it would be better if the Duchess did not see copious drops of blood staining the brown fabric.

"I assume she's upstairs, yes." Kathryn stared down her husband. "And I'm going up. You can come if you want, but don't try to tell me to calm down!"

"You of all people should know better." Matthew looked at the Duke's lovely sister, who was presently scowling at him.

"Of what do I stand accused, My Lady?" He was not in the mood to be upbraided and he had not kept Christine's injury from her sister. He had just not yet informed her.

"The moment she was injured, you should have sent for Kathryn," Cassandra said.

"Oh, so I should have left her and ridden for her sister while she bled? Or maybe I should have carried her on a horse across the fields instead of tending to her here and sending for the doctor?" The menace in his voice surprised a look of calculation in his unwelcome guest's eyes.

"Well, when you say it that way... I'm sorry. It is just that as soon as Kathryn heard she insisted racing over here. It was all I could do to at least get her to wait for the carriage. Michael would have had my head. He will anyway."

"And how did the Duchess hear of this unfortunate circumstance? I certainly did not send a rider that direction."

"I know, I believe one of our staff met the doctor's party on the way. Kathryn deduced Christine was in trouble when she could not get answers about her."

"I'm going to have to send her away," Matthew said.

"No." Michael reacted, his tone slicing the quiet.

"Ahhh, did I say that out loud?

"You did, you silly man and you know that will never do. First, there is nowhere for her to go and second, she wouldn't if you tried to make her."

"I could still try." He knew he had already lost the argument with the Duchess and her no-nonsense reply. He was surprised at Michael's reaction, but he knew the pair were not prepared for Christine to leave them just yet.

"Stop. Think. We will just have to protect her better."

"But she was with Michael..."

"Outside," his friend reminded. "At night."

"True. We will not do that again."

"I daresay when she is back on her feet you can devise some measures she will adhere to. I believe she is not as headstrong as her sister." The Duke cast a challenging glance at his wife who obviously chose to ignore the barb. "And of course, Kathryn will insist."

"You're right."

"Of course. Now, I believe there's a lady who will want to hear your voice."

Three days later, Christine had not fully regained consciousness. She had moaned and thrashed. She had winced in pain time and again until Matthew had lost count. But she had not opened her eyes. He was scared to death she never would.

He had used those days to search the woods from where the arrow was loosed. Churned tracks suggested the marksman stood his horse for hours waiting for his deadly opportunity. He had ridden in his own tracks back to the creek running through Weatherford and likely slipped away over the rocky track on the other side farther down the stream, leaving no further prints.

That they had not been able to follow the assassin's trail only confirmed their earlier suspicions. The old spy business Manseri had brought to them had to be settled before someone was killed.

He had thankfully not had to argue with the Duchess to keep Christine in his house. But he had realized why he had won that battle so quickly when the Duchess and a good number of her servants and other worthies had relocated themselves to his household. A prideful man might have been offended the Duchess and her staff felt the need to augment the amenities in his chambers and the offerings of his kitchen, but he was not such a man. His house was lacking and if Kathryn Stafford needed something to care for Christine, she could bloody well bring it in with her.

The advent of the Ducal servants had allowed him to make quick work of finishing the stables. He had plenty of chores to give them. His drinking well's rope and pulley mechanism was now working properly, his flower beds were tended and almost presentable, and there were certainly more things in his guest chambers.

"How are you feeling today, My dear?" Christine angled her head to the sound of the voice that had become so beloved to her these last days. She had made at least one decision while convalescing. She was going to stay here, and she was going to marry Matthew Drake, regardless of his circumstances or the danger to herself of being near him. The danger no longer mattered. She did not want to live without him. She would not live without him. And she knew beyond doubt he absolutely needed her.

"I still feel like I've been beat up. But on the bright side, I was awake enough to send Kathryn home for the day. I thought you might appreciate a little less activity in your house."

"I can be grateful for small favors. But, alas, she has tended you so well I have been able to get a great deal of work done around here." He paused, reached for a curl of her hair. "Bleu is missing you."

"Oh yes, how is she and how's the baby? I've been dying to get back out there. Oh, and what have you named him?" She slid her legs under her and beckoned him to sit.

"Minx, slow down and let me answer all of that. Mama's doing well. She's very attentive. Baby's been charming everyone and I haven't named him yet. It seemed fitting that you help me with it."

"Aww...thank you. I didn't expect to get to be part of it but if you are really considering ..."

"Absolutely. I want to hear what you have to say."

"I was thinking that in their family we have midnight, blue and stars—why not name him 'Sky'?"

"Sky. I like it. It's strong and bold. But he doesn't look much like a Sky? He's still totally black, not even one white sock." She watched the consideration in his intelligent eyes. Sitting with him, strategizing, sharing. What a partner she had found.

"Well, let's think. If Dad is Knight and a midnight color, hmmm... he could be Night Sky."

"Night Sky. Yes, that's it! You're a genius." When he grabbed her, clearly forgetting her barely healed state, she bit down on her lip to avoid gasping audibly. He was so happy. She was happy for him, for them. She would not let the pain shooting from her shoulder to her fingertips ruin this moment. Their moment. And in the future, there would be even more moments and for those she would feel better. But she knew there really was only one first colt. And she had named him or helped name him. No, she would not let Matthew see today how much the wound pained her.

"She still doesn't have use of her arm, Doctor." Matthew paced his study, while Michael stared intently at the doctor and Michael's lady passed him on her own circuit of his study.

"What are we not doing? She should have more use by now,

shouldn't she?" Kathryn asked Bridelsby. But they knew the answer, didn't they? Something was wrong.

"Your Grace, yes, I do believe she should have more motion and strength. But this was a deep and serious wound, so it's going to take some time. She's a tough little thing and there's no reason with time and care she cannot get back to her former self."

When Kathryn would have continued questioning Bridelsby, Michael sent her a look Matthew intercepted. The doctor had no more advice than he had the day before and Matthew was in no mood to continue to speculate. They needed a new strategy to help Christine progress. "My lord, I will call again tomorrow if it's all the same to you."

"Yes, thank you, Doctor. I will see you out."

"No, need, I know the way." He doffed his hat to Kathryn. "Your Grace."

Kathryn whirled on Matthew the minute the door closed behind the doctor. "Now, I think it's time we took Christine home."

"No!"

"No?"

"Yes, no. She can convalesce here. She wants to get out to the stables and she won't be able to see the colt if she leaves."

"But if she is at home, I will have many more ways to manipulate her into therapeutic activity."

"She can do your therapeutic activity here!"

"Yes, Matthew, you are correct. I can do therapy here." He cringed at the precise tone of his beloved as she regarded them icily from the doorway. But thankfully her cutting tone was not limited to him. "Kathryn, you can send all the therapy aids you want, but I have no desire to leave this house as long as the horses need me." *As long as Matthew needs me.* He was humbled to see her unsaid words in her eyes.

"My dear, you are dressed. Do you need to sit?" He reached a hand to assist her to the new chaise the Duchess had brought in that had replaced the one bloodied on the night of the shooting.

"I will sit. Thanks. And I want to continue discussing the subject I interrupted. What does the doctor say about my lack of progress?"

"With 'time and care', what we expect he would say and because he has absolutely no idea what else to do." Kathryn humphed and flopped into her husband's lap. "I know it's not proper and I'm sorry, but I just can't talk about Christy's injury any more without a little pick-me-up."

"For my part, I was ready to pull you over anyway. All of this anxious pacing is going to make the child a little demon."

The Duchess scowled at her husband then subsided into his arms.

"And we're back. No more depressing talk of my stupid shoulder's unwillingness to work. Instead, let's talk about how you are doing." Christine directed her attention to her now recumbent sister, who did look a bit flushed and pale all at once.

"I have to sleep with pillows all around me. My feet are swollen, and I have terribly unladylike cravings for meat and sweets in the night. But otherwise, I'm just awesome!"

She laughed at her sister. The smile was weak, but he thought it a real sign she might be improving after all.

She was worried. She could not hold her own coffee cup or brush her hair or dress herself without becoming exhausted lifting the cup, wielding the brush, or wrestling the fabric. She had no range of motion and almost any exertion shot pains to her fingertips, just as it had a week earlier when she had first woken from her coma. She had heard the whispered conversations in the hall. And the worried voices. She knew she was long past the time for showing improvement and was supposed to be much better by now.

Her training told her the wound itself was mostly healed. She could see very well the stitches had held. But whatever was wrong on the inside was still killing her. What was she supposed to be doing to exercise her arm, to relieve the excruciating pain, to regain her function? She scanned her room and her eyes landed on the brass door stopper. As she stooped to pick it up, she laughed at the subtlety with which her sister had managed to introduce all sorts of niceties to her host's home. She hefted the weight and curled it back to her bicep. She could do this. Breathe, pump, breathe.

Matthew watched Christine from her sitting room door. He had paced the hall wanting to talk to her to see how she was after their very frank discussion of her slow progress. He had decided to invite her to join him, although it was terribly improper for him to be in her domain. He did not believe she would be concerned.

She was unsurprisingly doing some exercise, wincing in pain, sweat beading her pale skin. As she swayed, he pounced. She allowed him to take her weight so he lifted her into his arms. Her bed had been turned down so he laid her gently on the sheets.

"Don't. Don't step away. We have to talk." She reached for him.

"You're exhausted. We can talk in the morning, when you've had time to rest." She had hold of his sleeve and pulled him toward her. He was not in the mood to resist but he knew he would have little control if she took this encounter farther than talk.

"Just crawl up here, please. I need a hug and I just want to be with you. Here in the quiet." He pulled off his boots, loosened his cuffs and dropped his waistcoat onto the chair next to her dressing table. He had the wherewithal to lock her bedroom doors, then slid under the sheets with her. She turned to him, burying her face in his chest. And she wept.

He knew she was tired and sore and worried over her slow convalescence. He suspected she might also be worried about him, the lurking dangers, his horses, and her sister's continued lethargy. He could not leave her. Sobs rocked her small form, even as he held her in the lee of his body. Not until her sobs slowed to hiccups and with the candles guttering, he gave up to the sleep of the truly exhausted.

The arrow had been far more effective than even he had dreamed. The girl had foundered, the family rallying to her side distracted, the sacred Duchess pulled and wan. The girl might even yet die of infection.

More. More of those tactics. A more toxic poison on the arrow perhaps?

8

———

She floated in warmth with an unfamiliar pressure across her chest and stretched in the delicious cocoon of her bed. Her eyes found the amber and rose highlights of the rising sun across the unshaven cheek of Matthew Drake. "Shhh...we can still avoid detection by the maids if I slip out now."

"Will you, can't you stay?" she whispered.

"I want very much to stay but I also want you to have a choice, to come to me because you have decided. Not because you were sad and sore, and we fell asleep. Let me go now to protect your reputation and we will...we will talk about this."

"Is it because I'm a virgin?"

"Argh. Of course it is. No...look at me." He touched her chin. "Oh, you are breathtaking all warm and snuggled. I have to go. But I will tell you." He took a deep breath before speaking again and looked her directly in the eyes. "I have never taken a woman either. When I do, it will be you and you will have made your choice. But now, I have to go down that back staircase." And he kissed her nose and pulled away.

He was still almost fully dressed. With amazing swiftness, he donned his boots, waistcoat and jacket. He was gone before she had come fully awake.

Matthew was already at his place at the breakfast table when she entered the room. She felt the heat rise in her cheeks. He smiled warmly, and she forced herself to return the greeting. There were too many other people about for her to suddenly succumb to blushing and stammering in his presence. Everyone would immediately think what almost happened but didn't, actually did.

"Your sister has not yet graced us with her presence. I thought you might like to drive over and see what's keeping her."

"Oh, I'd love to. Oh... I notice you said drive. Do you think I'm still not up to managing a horse?"

"Unfortunately, I doubt it. And don't get that look I know you're about to. You can manage the gig well enough and I will come along on Knight. He hasn't had proper exercise in several days."

"That's my fault. I'm sorry."

"Nonsense. I told you I've been busy rebuilding. Mostly inside, but we've gotten a remarkably lot done. Your convalescence has provided a good excuse to focus on chores close to home. But the brute of a horse is ready to run a little."

"I guess you'll be running circles around me then because I know the gig isn't actually going to go fast enough to give that big beast any kind of pace."

"Ha, no. I will do some trotting and we will of course have company to protect you."

"Notice, I'm not arguing about the extra muscle. Let me get on riding gear and I will meet you outside. Ten minutes?"

She had learned her guards' names and hailed McCaskill as he emerged from the kitchen door. If she was taking the gig, she would give the poor old cob Joey an apple treat. "Are you alone, no sidekick today?"

"Yes, miss. As his Lordship is also riding, we two should be able to handle the unforeseen. I sure am pleased to see you up and about."

"Oh, you cannot imagine how frustrating it is to be stuck in bed..." She trailed off at the twinkle in his knowing dark eyes. He was a soldier, of course he knew about wounds. "Have you ever been..."

The rest of the question died under the crashing of hooves in the forecourt. She was just in time to see Matthew, looking very much like the cavalry captain he had been, rein in the gorgeous black stallion. Would she always react like a schoolgirl with a crush on the quarterback when she saw him?

"Miss Ragland, I see you are ready."

"And I see you ran a few of the fidgets out of him before sticking him with my frumpy ride."

"Nonsense. He was happy for a few minutes of freedom, but he will be just as happy for the gallop across Asterleigh's land."

While they had calmed Knight, Hunter rolled up in the gig. "I think I best be riding along, miss. Just in case...you know."

"I do not plan to need your assistance in driving, but I will be happy to have your company."

"Then just pertend like I'm not here."

"Pretend."

"Yep, that miss."

As Christine sat in the gig, the hairs on her neck prickled, and she did not ignore the strange warning.

"Hunter, there's someone watching us. Don't turn around but see if you can see anything. Left shoulder, ten o'clock."

"I think the Captain's perked up too, miss. He's palmed his piece."

"Let's pick up our pace a little, I think. Our escorts will as well. If we're moving faster, I expect we will be a lot harder to hit." Joey responded to her gentle flick of the reins, just as the track widened on the edges of the property line.

"Christine. Whoever he is, he isn't following us onto Asterleigh's lands. But he's still watching. I want you to stay on this main. We won't take any of the shorter, narrower routes." Matthew's low-voiced commands matched perfectly with her own plan. She was not inclined to be shot again.

When the feelings of peril receded, she leaned back on the seat. Until that moment, when she relaxed, she had not realized how much the tension had tightened her arm muscles, almost to immobility once again." Hunter, can you come on up here? I'm going to need you after all."

While her youngest escort scrambled up onto the seat, Matthew's face hardened. She knew he felt responsible and he was still concerned. Well, if she was able to drive almost all the way to Hawthorne, then she was certainly much better than she had been eleven days ago.

Soon they arrived at the Duke's estate.

"Good morning, Christine. I'm glad you've come." The Duke who greeted them in his forecourt, handing her down from the gig, was wound up tight. She could feel tension radiating from him. Something was very wrong.

"What is it?" She held his arm tightly, stopping his progress. "Tell me before we go in."

"Pains, like they will be at the end. Strong. She simply doubled over and screamed."

"False labor. It can be." They were moving quickly toward the door. "They can stop on their own...in my time they can be stopped."

"Bridelsby has her in bed. Warmed. He's given her some willow bark tea. We put in a little brandy to relax her, to ease the contractions. She's...scared. I'll take you to her."

Useless arm muscles forgotten, Christine raced with the Duke, taking the stairs two at a time. The small conference in the hall outside Kathryn's suite stopped as the two women gaped at Christine's unladylike charge toward them and her sister's door. Kathryn's maid, Ellie, and housekeeper, Mrs. Staggs, looked back and forth at each other until Mrs. Staggs took what must have been a fortifying breath to speak to the Duke.

"She's had a little blood. He's got her in bed and she's stopped screaming with the fear. But he says it's likely just the liquor calming down the pain. But, he's got her more comfortable for sure."

"Thank you, Staggs. Ellie, I suspect you should stay, in case the doctor needs anything."

"Yes, Your Grace." And she nodded toward Christine. "I expect this one will be a welcome face for her." Her attempt at encouragement reminded Christine to paste on a smile.

"Thank you. Ladies, shall we?"

The room was sweltering, candles burned, and the fire made up to a virtual bonfire. Christine stared at her once fearsome, protective sister, and best friend propped on a mound of pillows deathly pale, sweating and breathing deeply. "Kat, open your eyes. I'm here."

"Oh, Christy. Stop it. Make it stop." As Christine moved to the bed, the doctor slipped into the shadows. Kathryn clenched her hand in a death grip. "It's all too soon."

"Shhh...calm down. You know stress will just make it worse." She slipped free of the tight grip, surreptitiously feeling for her sister's pulse. She counted to herself as Kathryn's eyes closed. "Relax, now, Sis. Let's get back to your breathing."

Christine felt the change in Kathryn's tension under the pressure of her hand. She also felt the stir of air from her brother-in-law's presence.

"Michael. Where are you?" Kathryn's summons bore little resemblance to her usually upbeat tone.

"Here, my love. Shall I sit with you?"

"Please, yes. Can you sit behind me?" He moved to comply as she spoke, giving Christine the opening to stretch her own stiff back and contemplate how she would manage to help stop the labor pains.

"Michael, why don't you rub her shoulders? And see if you can support her to sit a little more upright."

She had never noticed the clock on her sister's mantle, but settling in the chair near it, she watched the minutes tick loudly as her sister's breathing returned to normal and the tension visibly eased in the room.

"Your Grace, I think the worst is past." Christine had almost forgotten the doctor's presence until he spoke. "For these minutes now, the cramps have come further rather than closer." Dr. Bridelsby was moving back from the bed so Christine eased out of her chair to climb in at her sister's feet.

"Do you think? Ahem, what I, hmm... I'm wondering," stammering to a halt and flushing, Christine was grateful when the gentleman raised his palms out.

"I think yes, the worst is over. Your Grace, I'm going to check once more. Nothing much, just a little pressure."

"Okay, yes, please. I want...to know."

She followed Bridelsby to the door after his comforting words. She replayed them in her head. The pregnancy should continue and whatever had been passed was not life threatening. The cramps had largely stopped as had the bleeding, but Kathryn was now permanently confined to bed. He must have seen her expression because he added, "I'm sorry, miss, but I think it's the right decision for Her Grace for now. Closer to her time, we may be able to look at sitting up on the chaise but she's on her bed for now."

"Yes, we'll see that she stays in it. Thank you, Doctor, thank you so much."

"It's an honor to serve this household, miss. This Duke and Duchess have a lot of people counting on them."

She didn't wonder what he meant. She had seen first-hand how the Duke took care of everyone in the neighborhood—his friends, his tenants, the parishioners, and even the creatures. And she had heard the rumors about his careless predecessors. Before she could shut the door to Kathryn's room, she also heard a familiar male voice in the hall below.

She wanted to see him, to tell Matthew what had happened and to be held again. Passing Mrs. Staggs on the stairs, she asked the servant to let Kathryn know she would be right back. She just needed to talk to Matthew. She hurried toward him. "I heard your voice. I wanted to tell you."

"Yes, please, let's sit in here." He led her into the unused front parlor and pulled her onto the chaise beside him. "Now, tell me how she is. How they all are."

"She's stopped the contractions I believe but she's not out of the woods. She will be on bedrest for the remainder of her pregnancy."

"That's going to be difficult..."

Such an understatement. What it meant to Christine was equally difficult. She would have to move back into the Asterleigh household. No more stolen kisses, or scandalous sleepovers.

"Yes, on her but also on all of us. She will not be an easy patient, Michael won't want to leave her side and I...will need to be here. I'm sorry."

"Never be sorry. Kathryn's health, the baby, they are the most important right now. And I suspect while you are tending her, she will figure out how to help you with 'therapeutic' exercises as well."

"So true, we'll probably out boss ourselves. She may end up kicking me out. I'll have to come back to your house after all."

He tightened his grip on the hands he had grasped. "I will look forward to it."

"I've got to get back to her now though. I didn't really tell her I was leaving but for a minute." Matthew didn't have a choice. He had to let her go but dammit if he would do it without kissing her. Emerald eyes deepened to darkest lake water, her mouth sighed open and he touched his lips to hers. With her hands still caught in his own, he eased her arms around his back and freed one hand to hold her in place. The other slid into the mass of luxurious silken locks.

With her invitation clear, he slid his tongue into the glorious cavern of her mouth, reveled in her giving, the tangle of tongues. She tasted of life. Sweet, precious and rich.

They had spent the night together, embracing, but only now shared their first kiss.

"I'll bring your things in the morning, and check on Kathryn. For now, I will bid you adieu."

She let him walk out. She couldn't ask him to wait around, for the next time she could come down and see him. He had work and she was needed upstairs. But her resolve to marry Matthew Drake, newly-minted kisser extraordinaire, was firm. Soon. If he didn't ask her, then she was going to do it herself. She had a strong suspicion why he hesitated, and that male protectiveness would just have to take a backseat to her need to be his wife and partner.

Her righteous indignation carried her all the way back up the stairs to Kathryn's door where the large figure of her brother-in-law slumped. Michael saw her approach, reached his arms out and bear hugged her. She felt the warm tear slide down her cheek and soon her tears were melding with his and they were just two desperately scared people whose fears needed to be let free.

"I need to clean up and to give some instructions. You'll stay with her." Not a question from her emotionally-drained brother-in-law. "She's sleeping, I think."

The excellently oiled door eased silently open. Ellie worked her needle sitting on a rocking chair near the fire place. Kathryn breathed evenly and deeply.

"Why don't you take a break? I will sit with her a while and maybe then we can take turns when I stiffen up again," Christine whispered to the loyal maid. "I can't seem to make it through the day without becoming so tight."

"I wonder, miss, if that rub they use on the horses, you know for their aches and pains, might serve you."

"At this point I'll try anything. Can you sneak me a jar?"

"Aye, and I'll take my supper and bring you a tray."

"Deal. After I eat, I'll go wash, try the rub and then dig up some fresh clothes."

As Ellie started to leave, Christine thought of one more thing. "Maybe you could let Hallthorpe know His Grace could use a break for a brandy and a hot bath, too."

"Yes. I can do that."

In the haven of her own bedroom, Christine washed off the stickiness of sweat, then eyed the pot of salve warily. It smelled like home-brewed muscle relaxer and was going to make a terrible mess of her clean clothes. If there ever was a time for a sleeveless undershirt, this was it. She solved the problem by rubbing on only a small amount, saving the real treatment for once she dressed for bed. For now, she was clean and comfortable and feeling remarkably loose.

She made her way through the Duke's well-lit private domain to Kathryn's door and listened for any sounds. Hearing none, she slipped into the room. Ellie was once again at her post, this time working with lace and an evening gown. She signaled with her finger and made her way to the still figure on the bed.

"Christy, there you are," the voice raspy but strong.

"Hey, you too. When I saw you so still, I thought you were asleep."

"No, I was just pretending so Michael would leave and go bathe. Hallthorpe had gotten him to eat a little but he wouldn't take the time to get cleaned up and dressed more comfortably."

"He's been getting a little done. I know he had at least one meeting downstairs because I heard the coming and going. And I think he's got a scone on his desk for a snack."

"Yes, Mrs. Staggs made him promise to have something since he didn't eat very much of what she put on his tray. I think there were some words exchanged."

"He's worried. He's a man and a frightened Dad. He can't help you so he's even more frustrated."

"So now he thinks I'm asleep and is ideally now getting a bath. We have to keep whispering because he's only two doors away. If he hears us..."

"Count on me, big sis. I can whisper if you can. Now, whisper to me how you are. What do you feel like?"

"Honestly, I feel like I've been run over by a Mack truck. Everything hurts."

"I'm sorry. We probably loaded you with a little too much brandy. That's why your head hurts."

"My head does hurt, but likely as much from the screaming and the passing out. Did you know I hit the floor?"

"Oh, no. No wonder everything hurts. You're hung over, bruised and had hard labor pains."

"But for all everything hurts, feel this." She took Christine's hand and guided it over the mound of her belly, pressing their joined hands to her side. They waited. And she felt it. The flutter, and then the gentle ripple, the very real movements. The baby was moving. "He, or she, is still alive and being able to feel that is distracting me from how lousy the rest of me feels."

"It's amazing. Just there. He, or she sure did give us a scare. And on that subject, let's talk about the rules."

"The rules. Oh great, all those years I bossed you around are coming back to haunt me. Well, as the English say, do your worst."

"One word, sis, bed."

"Bed?"

"Yes, bedrest indefinitely I'm afraid. Until the doctor says otherwise, but likely until you are close enough timing is inconsequential."

"Well, I don't know what else I expected. Surely, I won't have to have this pillow under my butt for the whole time. I think all the blood's drained out of my feet and legs."

"Let's move that one and make you more comfortable. Can I check and be sure you're not bleeding? Though you'd feel it, right?"

"I think so, I felt it before, I mean. The warm flow. It horrified me. I screamed from the pain and the blood. You'd have thought I was being killed the way everyone raced in here. And I hit the deck about the time Michael got to the door. He picked me up and when he realized what was wrong he started shouting for guards because he thought I'd been injured."

"You probably looked pretty bad. I hate the two of you had to go through that."

"I see you are not asleep after all."

The much more composed Duke of Asterleigh, looking very much the Lord of the manor with crisp white shirt, buff breeches and a loose necktie eased from the doorjamb. His mock scowl belied by the twinkle in his eyes.

"I've been visiting with my sister. Oh, Michael, come. Here, let me have your hand." Christine eased away from the bed as Michael took her spot. His large hand she guided to Kathryn's belly and Christine watched the wondrous expression spread across his face. His relief was palpable when he too knew their child lived.

She was definitely de trop. Christine slipped from the room and went in search of Ellie who she realized had also retreated. Finding the maid in the kitchen she filled her in on Kathryn's status. The baby was alive. Her tension had largely receded and ensuring Ellie would be waiting to take Michael's place in Kathryn's room, she slipped out into the kitchen garden. The air was too crisp for much deep contemplation, but the walled garden's rich earthy scent eased the last of her current tension and fears. She opened her mind, to think of her own problem. How could she convince Matthew to propose to her? *When you decide to come to me.*

Come to me. Could it really be that simple?

How she would actually manage to go to Matthew took considerable time and planning. Between the very real threats to her safety and her sister's lingering ill health, Christine spent the better part of a week searching for the elusive opportunity. When she found the opening, it was in fact all rather easily done.

"Michael, Your Grace, excuse me."

Her formidable brother-in-law looked up from the papers he was studying to regard her with those shrewd brown eyes.

"I would like to visit the horses. It's been a week since I've examined the colt and ridden Fleur. And, in truth, I would like to check on Lord Worley."

"Check on, as in make sure he is eating his vegetables?" He lifted a brow.

"Something like that. I think he would work too hard if we weren't watching out for him." *And I need to see him. To let him know how I feel.*

The unspoken words must have been reflected in her own eyes because he asked no more. Rising and coming around the desk, he stood closely to her, looked down into her eyes and his warmed.

"You have been a godsend to me during these last days. I don't know what Kathryn, or I would have done without you. I will grant your request under one condition."

She eyed him warily. "What is it?"

"You have committed in your heart to staying here?"

"Yes..."

"Then you know that some decisions are irrevocable?"

"I'm not sure to what you are referring but I know there's no going back, if that's what you mean."

"Yes, that's what I mean." She was extremely grateful he let it go at that. She was afraid he could guess exactly what she planned. And she did not want to contemplate anyone knowing the full truth until she had convinced Matthew she wanted to be his. She wondered, not for the first time, how hard that would be.

Matthew saw them when they were still far enough away for him to steel his features and wrestle his attraction to the woman into something manageable. Not manageable in fact. She was like a disease. He had been desperate to see her, practically moping through his days one minute and throwing himself in to hard labor the next. That she was riding onto his land just as his need for her had become almost an obsession...

"It's the horse doctor," he hailed her and her escort.

McCaskill also accompanied by his partner, Rose, halted a few paces beyond them, affording Matthew the chance to help Christine from her saddle. She was clad inappropriately in her riding pants with a loose white shirt and smart-looking jacket. Of course, she looked delectable with her luscious bottom encased in the figure-hugging fabric. He bit down on his bottom lip.

"To what do we owe the pleasure?"

"I'm glad you think so. That it's a pleasure, I mean. I was just... dying to see the colt," and you. She left the last unsaid with words but hoped her eyes conveyed her strong desire to be with him. "Am I interrupting?"

"No, I was just about to check on the pair of them. I think Mama's missed you."

"Oh, I've missed her. I know I've been helping and very needed at Kat's bedside, but how I've wanted to see how much he's changed and how she's recovering."

As they moved into the cool barn, her eyes adjusted to the lower light and she heard the rustling from several horses. How much she had needed to be here in this barn, where they had met, to initiate this next phase of their relationship.

Matthew led her down the line of stalls to where the colt and his lovely mother were comfortably nuzzling. "Oh look at him. He's just stunning. And so incredibly solid black."

"Not a mark on him and already showing signs of his bloodline. He's going to be a menace if he's even somewhat as fast as his sire. You know he will be sought after," Matthew said.

She turned to look at Matthew. "But can you manage to part with him?"

"I might not have a choice. While I am loath to admit it, he might be just the thing to rescue this estate. I have to consider it."

"I'm sorry. I can tell you are torn by the thought."

"Not as much as I am determined to make a go of this place. Come, let me show you something."

He led her back to the empty office and picked up the open ledger from the desk. "What is this? These look like racing times." She looked from the page back to him, excitement building. She did not know much about racing times, but she expected these were good.

"I never thought of Knight as a racer. He was always destined to be my cavalry horse. But when we first ran him...well these are really good times. Probably not quite competition times but they're good enough to add to Sky's list of antecedents. I just need someone to time him in an official setting. And I need a jockey for that."

"A jockey, huh?"

"Why do you have a look in your eye?"

"You know I could do it. And I wouldn't cost you a thing."

"First of all, stop that." She was jumping up and down for joy and more and holding him in the empty office of the barn in which they had met so many weeks ago. She had worn the green lace underwear for luck and as she laughed with joy over his befuddled look, she also felt his interest and arousal. She slowed her movements and pressed herself to the front of him. He sucked in a breath. She knew when his eyes narrowed, the exact moment he realized she was looking at him with interest—sexual interest, and arousal. "You need to let go of me Christine."

"I think I will not actually." Then he did try to pull away. She thought, believed, it was only a half-hearted effort. So she leaned fully against him and kissed his throat and found his wildly beating pulse point as erratic as her own. Taking that as a good sign, she licked, and suckled his neck.

His arms came around her and he was lost. Lost in the smell of her, the feel of her, the life of her. He buried his face in her glorious mane of hair and gave up resisting. He pushed her shoulders back. She leaned against his palms and seemed to say, 'I'm ready'. No force on earth could tear him from his woman, willing, ready. He turned her back to the desk and lifted her by her bottom onto its relatively clean surface.

Eyes level, he took her mouth. The kiss grew, deepened until their breaths mingled, the sounds and smells were only of her and her feminine musk. He gentled the kiss to pull away enough to slip his hands between their bodies and over her shoulders to slide the riding jacket from her.

The jacket fell forgotten to the rough floor as she threaded her hands in his hair and deepened the kiss again, to a new plane, a new awareness. His trembling fingers went to the buttons of her white blouse. The halves fell open, he pushed them wide, wider, then slid his hands down her arms. As the garment dropped away, he was amazed anew at the lean loveliness of her skin, the glorious beauty of her. He had no words.

She must have sensed his hesitation because she guided his hands to the waist band of her breeches. They trembled only slightly. Together they slipped the buttons free. She slid off the table so he could kneel to pull off her boots and the tight fitting pants. He tasted her knee, and the strong slim thigh, trailing his tongue up the length of her until he was once again towering over her. She reached around his neck and he lifted her again.

She wriggled against the back of the desk at the same time allowing her legs to fall open. He stepped between them fitting her most intimately to his still-clothed front. He wondered fleetingly if he could be with her without taking her virginity. Was there a way to protect her from being irrevocably tied to him? She answered his question by pressing closer to his arousal.

He moved against her, she answered with mewling sounds completely undoing the last of his control and stealing that last sane thought. He had always been able to control his sexual urges at school, on Campaign and once he was out of the service and thrust into the social world. He could not do so with her. He slipped his hand between them startling another satisfied moan from her while he opened the placket of his trousers. He pressed close once again and she tilted her hips. Her eyes closed, and a small line of concentration formed between her brows.

He took control moving in ever so slightly to her tightness and out gently. The mewling turned to panting and he thrust to seat himself fully. She gasped and clung to him. Her maidenhead had been all but a spider's web, and he fleetingly contemplated that it must be for all of the years of her riding and other athletic pursuits. He held her until her breathing melded with his, then he began to move. When she began to tighten around him, he pressed deep, breathed in the womanly smell of her musk mixed with another feminine floral scent and gave himself to her.

Eventually, she returned to the world of the living with slowing breaths. Horses shifted and snorted and somewhere outside a stable hand called to another. She watched him for some sign that he was satisfied with her decision. He was staring at her with questioning eyes. "Are you okay?"

"I am. I guess we had better show our faces. Folks will eventually begin to wonder."

His rueful expression worried her. Had she not pleased him? Or, had he been sorry they made love? She wasn't fool enough to think he had not enjoyed it. But she knew his stubborn pride. She had goaded him into it and he was looking at her with the guilty look that said he was not yet convinced they could or would marry. She would show him.

She was tucking her shirt into her waistband when she heard Hunter call for her. "In here. Lord Worley is showing me the log of Knight's track times."

Matthew had taken a seat to pull on his boots and right the rest of his clothes. They had only seconds before Hunter would join them. She stepped out into the aisle as Hunter stopped to acknowledge the great horse. The giant head nudged his hand and the young man laughed. The crash surprised them all and Christine turned on her heel, charging at the open office door.

A befuddled-looking Matthew stood in the midst of several broken pots with an amount of goo over his front. "I did not mean to pull the entire shelf down. I was looking for the salve for your shoulder. I understand, Miss Ragland, that the horse salve has worked wonders on your injury."

"Thank you, Lord Worley, it has. Can we help you clean up this mess?" She was trying desperately not to laugh. He must have intentionally spilled animal salves on himself to cover up their recent activities. Should she also need to smell of horse medicine to mask the very human odors? Playing this game with him was going to be wonderful. She slipped a little in a particularly oozy puddle and then compounded the mess by splashing hard in another one to stop her slide.

Hunter's laughing started them both giggling and it took them much longer than necessary to get the mess off the packed ground floor. Once they had largely contained the disaster, she certainly did not smell like she had just had sex.

He had bedded Christine. Not bedded exactly, but taken her, compromised her. He would have to marry her if anyone found out or there was...heaven forbid, a child. But until then, he would do everything he could to protect her from being bound to him and Worley and its spate of dangers and troubles.

He watched her with Hunter talking about what it would mean to the estate if Knight was recognized as a thoroughbred stud. What Night Sky could mean to the estate. The two conspirators were clearly talking where he could hear them exclaiming the colt would surely need to stay here. He overheard their assessment he was far too valuable as an asset for the stud rather than as a commodity. They could dream all they wanted but he knew selling the colt might be one of the few means he had of staving off the financial ruin hovering over him.

Then there was the matter of her safety. He had to trust she was safe in Asterleigh's care because he could not protect her himself unless she was in arm's reach. And after their interlude today, he knew he could not risk her being close and doing that again. He fervently hoped this one indiscretion would not have consequences, because if they remained in close proximity he knew the temptation to be with her again and again would be too great.

"Lord Worley, what do you think of our idea?" She beckoned him to join them and he feigned incomprehension. Her eyes twinkled.

"Idea?"

"Yes, consider entering Knight in one of the local races. See how he does with competition? Someone mentioned that Christmas exhibition race. It's right around the corner."

"I hadn't thought of it, but you know as well as I Knight is really not a racer. He's never been in that particular situation. I can't imagine how he'd react to the other horses, not to mention the crowd."

"He's a war horse. I imagine he would react like the professional he is to the horses and noise," she replied.

She had a point. He was incredibly reliable in harrowing situations. A race would likely be not much different.

"You two have an interesting idea. We will think about it, and yes, we can research possible races." She smiled, with her glorious green eyes and her whole face, and he knew he was a man condemned. No, he would definitely not be able to stay away from her. Now that he had lain with her, knew her feel, her smell, knew she made those wonderful soft mewling moans, he would need her again and again. And he would not be able to contemplate her marrying anyone else.

So he would have to keep her safe in the meantime, be more judicious in their encounters to avoid getting her with child, solve all of his financial problems and destroy his elusive enemy. Then he could marry her properly.

With the Christmas race upon them, he was not any happier with the conspirators who had pulled him and his horse and his reputation into the idea of racing. That he had had no choice but to let Christine train Knight over these weeks made no never mind. She had allowed no objection and his usually reliable friend, Michael Stafford, had been unusually silent on the subject of his sister-in-law. He wondered fleetingly what Michael would say about the tryst between them. Thankfully the activity had not been repeated. He needed more time.

The tampering in the stables had finally stopped. That bridles and stirrups had been loosened, a burr placed on a saddle, had been annoying and particularly consistent. But with the advent of his visitor and his additional guards, they had finally been able to keep up their vigilance at all hours.

But that his elusive enemy was still actively working to destroy his stables he had no doubt. This run before Saturday's race would be Christine's last for some time. He was determined to relax and watch the woman and horse fly together in their final training run. But the prickling of the hairs on the nape of his neck told him all was not well. As Christine leaned into the sleek neck for the race to the tape, he saw her flinch, and her right foot slipped free of the stirrup. He watched in horror as the stirrup gave and her leg slipped as well. She sat hard onto the saddle and Knight checked his pace.

Clearly unprepared for the horse's move, Christine jerked forward. His heart in his throat, Matthew willed Knight to maintain control over his movements at that speed. In answer to his prayers, his remarkably well-trained horse slowed as it took the corner. He was racing to them and caught Christine as she slid from the saddle in a near swoon.

He steadied her on her feet as she lurched onto the churned track. Then she leaned back against him. There was no way to prevent the several onlookers from seeing she had been badly affected by the ride. He contemplated what this sudden weakness could mean. He was not going to be able to avoid the speculation. He did not want to think about that. For now, he had to get her inside and deal with the obviously tampered with horse and calm the grooms. And he had to prepare for a visit from his friend.

"Are you feeling better?" She turned to the sound of her big sister's voice at the door.

"I am, thank you. That was a wild ride and with the stirrup slipping…"

"I am sure it was but that is not what I am referring to." Kathryn came further in to her room, but she had not yet looked directly at her. She did not want to see condemnation in Kathryn's eyes and she was surely determined not to get a talking-to. Not now. And not if it meant discussing her very personal business.

She looked then and saw nothing but concern on her sister's pale and lovely face. "Should you be out of bed? I'm the one who should be checking on you."

"Ha, maybe. But I slipped out. I won't be up long. And I'm so stiff and sore from being bedridden I have been moving around a little. And it's almost Christmas Day and I haven't even seen the first Christmas decoration being cooped up on this floor."

Seeing her sister for the first time in weeks fully upright, she declared, "You're huge. I had not realized, you've been laying down, and..."

"Oh, yes, I'm sure it's because I've been laying down. I can't imagine how hard I'm going to have to work to get all the baby weight off. But you're talking about me to avoid talking about you."

"I'm not ready to talk about it."

"I don't think you have a choice after what happened today."

"What happened is I had a wild ride."

"What happened is you were almost thrown from a tampered with horse in front of several people and you swooned. There will be speculation about the horse and the swooning." She raised a brow at her sister's suggestion then slipped her arm around Kathryn.

"I'm not ready to talk about the swooning but I can talk about the horse."

"How about I ask this way?" Kathryn said calmly while gently stroking her hair. "If there was another reason for the swooning than the wild ride, would it require you to get married?"

The tears started then, and she didn't answer. Kathryn continued stroking her hair and her back, waiting for her answer. "I don't know for sure. It's been about three weeks since we... And I didn't mean to... I mean, I did but I didn't plan..."

"I think I understand. It's okay. Let's do the math and really embarrass you." Kathryn counted on her fingers. "Three weeks since sex would be five weeks since the start of the last cycle. You must be a little late?"

"This is not an enjoyable subject to discuss...even with your favorite sister. But oh all right yes, if we look at it like that I'm a little late but you know that's only a few days."

"But since it is possible, and this is the 19th century, you don't have much choice but to get out in front of it, Christy."

"I have to tell Matthew. I can't imagine what he must think. How... how will I tell him?" She hiccupped.

"After you practically fell into his arms, and since he was party to the activities, I suspect he already knows. That's probably why he's downstairs right now talking to Michael."

"Oh my, no, Michael... Argh." She tried to pull away, to run downstairs.

"Stop. Let's get you cleaned up and put a fresh dress on. You can go down when you're composed. I'm pretty sure he isn't going anywhere."

It took longer than she would have liked to get herself presentable. She knew she was pale and splotchy and she was mortally embarrassed. Thankfully, she had met no servants in the hall. Michael's office door stood ajar. She must have made some sound because the cavalry officer she had very possibly made a baby with turned from the garland-draped fireplace where he had been staring into the coals. At the sight of her he smiled, tentatively. She could read only concern in his expression. He came to her and pulled her more fully into the room. "Are you feeling better?"

He stroked the back of one cool hand down her burning cheek. She closed her eyes and could not prevent the escape of another tear. He leaned over and kissed it gone.

"I am. I cleaned up and I didn't..."

"Have another episode?" he asked, lifting her chin with one strong finger. He kissed her lips, just a whisper and she sank against him.

Holding her now he felt so much calmer than he had as he had sorted her out and handed Knight over to the stable hands who had come running. He had gone through the motions of helping Christine into the gig and sending her off with Rose and McCaskill. They too had eyed him suspiciously. He wasn't sure if it was because she had been endangered or because of her overly strong reaction to the horse's actions. She should have been able to handle a slip like that. He suspected they were both a little in love with their charge. Who wasn't? He certainly had no qualms about what he was about to do next.

"Christine, are you...with child?"

She jumped, then slumped again. "I don't know. I could be, maybe, but it's too soon to know, right," she whispered against his chest.

"It's going to be okay. Regardless, we will be married."

"What?"

"Married. We will marry right away. I will give you the protection of my name."

She raised her perfect little nose at him. "We...will...be...married."

"Yes. I have a special license."

"Wait. You already have a license?" She shifted fully away from him and jerked around to face him. Her stance was not encouraging. Her next works stung. "You assumed I would marry you, so you just got a license, all on your own?"

"You offered yourself to me. As a gentleman..."

"A gentleman. A gentleman! Oohh!!" She stomped to the still-open door and down the hall. He was absolutely sure that had not gone well.

9

$\mathcal{I}$ do believe, my friend, that you did that worse than I when I proposed marriage to the elder Ragland sister. I believe I spouted some drivel about Kathryn doing a good job as a Duchess and bearing me children. I should probably have warned you that a business proposal would not garner you a positive outcome."

His closest friend was sitting there as smug as you please while he had his first proposal thrown in his face. Well, not proposal exactly. Maybe it had been less of a question and more of an order. Argh. No wonder she had balked. He had talked to her like the veriest green Lieutenant.

"I believe I will need to make up some lost ground. Advice, my friend?"

"Tell her why you want to marry her. Aside from the obvious for which she seems to be a bit embarrassed. Because she means something to you."

"Feelings. Not a currency I have dealt in for some time." The tension that had started the moment Christine Ragland had stomped out was fading from his neck and he took the seat across from

Michael's desk. "Let's talk about her circumstances for a moment before I chase down my intended bride."

"Naturally, Kathryn will want to have the wedding here. As she cannot leave the house anyway, all should expect it."

"Thank you. I believe something small will do but I do not want to deny her her day."

"I am sure Kathryn and Christine will devise something they can both live with."

"I know you are well aware I cannot in good conscience claim funds I do not have. In fact, I received another..." His friend held up a staying hand.

"I was planning to tell you at some point once we had settled the problems. Nevertheless, it will be now. I and a small group of 'investors' have been seeking out Seb's vowels to reclaim them. I for one was not having you lose Worley."

"Michael, what have you done? I never asked, never meant..."

"You don't usually stutter either my friend." His childhood friend, partner in high adventures, closest confidante was offering him, no giving him without asking, a freedom he had not dared hope would come for years and with much more work. "I wanted to, always intended to. First, you are the Baron of Worley. No one else. Second, I suspected, or more hoped, the debts were not as they seemed. Now we know the truth I can negotiate the remaining amounts down even further. No one who holds a voucher under those circumstances will be able to claim the debt is entirely legitimate. Whoever was driving you into debtor's prison has to know by now that he will not take Worley by that means."

"I will not reply with the ungracious 'you should not have' or even that I will repay you, because I do not know when I ever will. But I will try, and I hope that's good enough."

"You will repay only the portion upon which we agree and some of it will be a dowry for Christine. I can do that. I will do it as her brother-in-law."

He shook his head, disbelief mixing with relief and bone-deep gratitude. "You do not have to gift any of it."

"I do, and I will. We will agree on terms when the solicitors get here. We can set some of it aside as a permanent fund for her and your children."

"I am not so stubborn that I will continue to argue with a Duke who is sitting behind his very imposing desk with that look of authority." He laughed at the absurdity of what was happening and maybe with a little joy.

Michael relaxed, and he decided it was time to change the subject.

"Let's talk about her safety. I am concerned the attacks on her will intensify. The saddle spurs, the cut stirrup...those weren't ultimately dangerous. But the arrow, that could have killed her. And now with the possibility of..." A baby. There would be a child to protect in the midst of all of the chaos of his life. He felt the blood drain from his face.

"Whoa, my friend. Be at ease. We will work through all the security measures we need to keep Christine safe."

"I didn't mean for this to happen, not now. I wanted to wait, until all the troubles were behind me and I could come to her whole, someone she could be proud of. You've given me my freedom back but there is still so much uncertainty."

"Matthew. I've known you all my life. You are the hardest working, most upstanding man I know. She will be proud and honored to have you. Just do a little better with the question and let's plan a wedding!"

He understood her. She would be in the stables, talking to one of her precious mares, complaining about boneheaded men. Then she would listen because that's who she was. "You are as predictable as me."

She turned her gaze to his and continued to stroke the silky brown head. "They are excellent listeners."

"And I am a clod. Christine, let me try again?" He took her hand and pulled her fully around to face him. He held her green gaze and took a deep breath. "The moment I saw you, I knew you were trouble. And also, somehow, I knew you were mine. I had waited, you understand what I mean, for the right person. I resisted my attraction to you as long as I could. I believe it was you who precipitated our next step." She blushed gloriously. And she was listening intently. He was obviously doing this much better than the first time.

"I waited too. And I just sort of...knew."

"Yes." He tightened his grip on her hands. "You were right. Our time has come. I am not sure about all of the troubles that are plaguing us, but I am sure we will work together. I am determined to keep you safe and I will worry about you and..." She bit her lower lip and a light blush stained her cheeks once again. "I am thrilled about even the idea there may be a baby. And scared to death."

"I'm so sorry. I didn't mean to, I didn't try to..."

"Stop that, Christine. If we made a child, we will know soon. And we are going to keep him or her safe. Period. And we are going to marry. Acceptable? Soon?"

"Okay, yes. Soon."

"Good." He pulled her in to his body. And he saw the movement, just a break in the light. He tossed her to the ground and fell into a low crouch as the arrow whizzed past just overhead. It landed in the straw in the stall of the lovely mare Christine has been stroking. And promptly burst the pile into flame. "Christine, stay down. We've got to get this horse out and I've got to go after him."

"I'll help you with the horse and the fire, but you are not going after him."

He had the stall door unlatched so the spooked horse bolted for the aisle. Thankfully, someone whipped the stable door open and the fleeing horse kept running. Then there were more people and buckets of water handed to him. And other doors flung open with horses clambering to escape the melee. The flames were hot, but the straw was burning itself out. Hands reached, tossed, dirt and water mixed, splashed onto stall walls, the floor.

Somewhere in this thick of the danger were Christine, who might be carrying his unborn child and an assassin.

He tossed the water from the bucket in his hands and fell back to the aisle. He saw her then, through the door stroking the now calm mare. And he saw the body. He had not heard a shot but there on the ground lay a man, darkly clad, with a quiver of arrows at his side, a slow trail of bright red leaking into the dust from a fatal wound in his side.

"Do we know him?"

"No," answered Michael, who was part of a circle guarding the body. He had not even noticed the others. McCaskill and Rose were there, clearly preventing Christine from looking too closely. "I've sent a rider to Weatherford. He can help us deal with this one. If he's a denizen of London's crime underworld, Julian will find him. There's no identification, but he has to have been staying somewhere. He must have been our archer."

"How did an assassin carrying a quiver get into our stable undetected? You have more people watching than I?" He heard the edge in his voice and as he saw Michael's jaw harden he did not care.

"As you say. Let's walk a moment, if you please. I have instructions for those two to be close but not to crowd her unnecessarily. Obviously, they knew something was going on. I doubt they suspected someone had been lying in wait in the barn. Clearly, he had. But their quick reactions and the lethal knife throw were perfectly placed."

"We don't believe this is over, with his death, do we?" He jerked his shoulder to the grotesque shape lying in the view of the house.

"No. But having him should give us some peace, if even for a moment. We should try to contain word of the death. Let's get him loaded on a cart and send him to Julian with all speed. Maybe his employer will have to deal with the small delay in attacking us while he is replacing him. "

"And give us time for a quick wedding?"

"Yes. This Saturday?"

"Saturday is the race."

"And then Christmas. What about a Christmas Eve wedding?"

"Yes. So just over a week. That's at least one thing I can control." At the raised eyebrow of his friend, Matthew shook his head. "Of course, I can't control that. But I can damn well ask!"

"Christmas Eve?" Matthew and Christine were marrying Christmas Eve, in a few days and with a race between? Kathryn narrowed her eyes at her husband. "What are you not telling me?" Christine caught the last sentence and laughed. How her brother-in-law would avoid telling his wife that another attempt had been made on her life, on his own land, she was unsure. But she knew he would try to evade.

"You agreed they need to marry."

"Yes, but in eight days. Surely we can have another week or two, to sew a new dress at least?"

"I believe, Michael, you better tell her all of it," Christine said, slipping in to the room. The hazel eyes darted from her to him speculatively and returned to rest on her sister's husband. "The staff is going to be whispering. Or I can tell you, sis."

"There was another attempt on her life."

"Christine? What happened? Are you okay?" Kathryn launched at her and grabbed her hands.

"Yes, don't freak. I'm okay. Everything's okay. This time, the assassin is dead, and I believe Lord Weatherford is taking charge of investigating him."

"Yes, Julian has contacts in London even I do not know. If this man is anyone at all Julian will find him. Maybe this time he can make a connection to the employer. And, the reason for the very hasty marriage can be blamed on the issue of her safety and keeping Christine in Matthew's company at all times. She will be safest sleeping in his bed."

"And they believe that it will take a little time for word of the assassin's disappearance to reach his employer. Maybe long enough for us to pull off an assassin-free wedding."

"Well then, Christmas Eve it is. I won't have to plan two separate menus. And I assume we won't be expecting Julian to return? We can send word to Hamilton. Are there others you would like to include?"

"We can let Mrs. Stogwell accompany the vicar."

"She will not approve, but yes."

"I will work on the list." Kathryn leaned over her husband's chair and kissed the top of his head. Michael sighed. Christine watched as the tightness in his jaw eased. His arm snaked out to catch his wife and Christine took that as her cue to slip back out of the room as quietly as she had entered.

She wondered if Matthew was still here and if he could finish his lovely proposal. He had not declared his love. Had he been planning to? Or was he not in love with her? Did it really matter at this point? He was marrying her because he had always thought of her as his and very likely gotten her pregnant or at least took her virginity which was almost the same since their honor required English Lords to marry girls they deflowered.

And he was likely not one of those English Lords who would set up a mistress. He couldn't afford to anyway.

He watched her drift out through the music room doors into the twilight pulling the shawl tightly around her. Did she know how vulnerable she looked hugging her waist and what might be their child? He winced. His fear was so real.

Did she even know where she was going? She was distracted. The day had been horrible. No wonder she wanted the peace of the outdoors and the terrace he knew lay just beyond. He followed her to the opening and scraped his shoe on the flags. She flinched but did not turn to him. "I believe you accepted my proposal before we were interrupted?" He came up behind her and pulled her against his chest. "Yes?"

"Yes. Thank you for doing it all over again. Your words were lovely."

"You deserved a proper proposal. I daresay you still have not really had a complete one. I intended to say the day you came into my life was the best one until then and each day continues to be better and better."

She leaned fully against him. "And that's even lovelier. I promise to try to be a good English wife. I'm sure it won't always be easy but like you, I knew from very early on you were the one I had been fated for."

"If there ever was a hand of fate certainly hers has been in our lives. The miracle that brought you and your sister to us, some days I still cannot fathom it." He shook his head and tightened his grip around Christine's waist.

"You know. It's probably almost easier for us because we saw the before. Or maybe the better description is we've seen both sides. And to some extent we know the magic formula that got us here."

"I have not really asked you what you think is the cause. Tell me."

"It's the portraits. There's a series and Kathryn took home the first one. Somehow, she must have dreamed herself into the time and place it happened. They're the key, but how they became magic time machines we don't know. For me getting here, I followed her trail. I had done that several times before but this time I literally tracked her movements to the minute including sitting at her desk and leaving at her exact quitting time. When I got to the shop, Ms. Tilly was so sweet. She wanted me to have the portrait of you. Even then the portrait spoke to me this time as it never had before. I would have bought it if she had not given it to me free of charge."

"Ah, yes. The one of me that Kathryn sent you the message on, that you were so determined to hunt up in my study."

She blushed prettily as he caught her. "Yes, but the message didn't survive over time. It was just when I saw it here in your time and place, with the paper backing still intact that I read her words. That was when the jig was up on you guys keeping us apart."

"We have talked about why Michael was so cautious. I think now that I have you, and what we have together, I understand fully his concern. He was not nearly as afraid of her leaving voluntarily as he was of her disappearing the way she arrived. I believe he still lives with the fear."

"I don't blame him. I don't want to leave you all, but we have never seen the process work in the other direction. I believe we're safe from it reversing"

"Promise me..." She turned in his arms at his pained voice, a look of concern marring her delicate features. He must have sounded especially morose. "...that if anything happens, you will do all within your power to return to me."

"Deal."

They stood embracing until she shivered ever so slightly. He reluctantly released her and turned toward the house, but she took his hand and stopped him. "Matthew? I want you to know, except for being mortally embarrassed that everyone knows my, our business, I am happy. Genuinely happy. No regrets. Understood?"

"Understood."

Then she let him lead her back in through the darkened room, but she did not release his hand. The hall was blessedly empty of servants and she kept her grip as she ascended the stairs. He knew he should not allow it, but he was not ready to release her. For no other reason than ensuring she was safe in her chamber he could go with her.

"I don't know what the protocol is about sleepovers once you're engaged but I really don't want to be alone tonight."

"It has been a trying day. I believe I can wake up before the servants and find my way out."

"No alarm clock, huh?"

"Alarm clock?"

"Yes. In my time, you can actually set the clock to ring at a specific time to wake you up."

"Ahh. I don't need an alarm clock, I have my own secret alarm."

"What, the rooster?" He was laughing as she drew him into her chamber. She shut the door with a glorious smile on her face.

"Well the rooster would likely wake me up but it's not as mysterious, or funny. I'm accustomed to campaigning and I naturally wake up before dawn. It's the cavalry in me." She was pulling him toward the settee by her cheery fire and he was rapidly forgetting about dawn.

"Stay with me then if you feel comfortable. Or even if it's just a little bit uncomfortable. My reputation is already ruined anyway." Then she kissed him as they tumbled in a tangle of arms and legs onto the bed. She held him as he turned to range over her. She was so gorgeous, so alive, so his. Had he ever believed, after the devastation wrought in his family and to his future to have her, to have this brightness for himself? He determined to savor her.

"That was amazing," Christine exclaimed.

"Second place. Don't that beat all?" Jem wondered aloud and

hugged his jigging wife amid the celebrants thronging around them. "And you even won some money Christine."

"I won a few coins but oh, Cassandra, did you bet on him too?"

"Of course I did. I bet on him to place and look at me." She jingled the coins in her reticule. "More Christmas presents."

Christine and Cassandra followed Jem as he pushed through the boisterous race crowd filled with everyone from farmers to local gentry. No one stopped them to speak or even congratulate them on the horse's success. Maybe no one knew of her or Jem and Cassandra's connection to Knight. Or maybe no one wanted to talk to her.

Cassandra was undaunted by the lack of attention they received and placed a loud smacking kiss on her husband's flushed cheek just as Michael joined the three of them in the carriage announcing, "Matthew's ready. Rose and one of his hands are with him."

"I saw Franks was finishing up with Knight. Rose was watching protectively. Are we not waiting on Matthew?" Christine asked.

"No, he's going to collect his winnings and talk to the guild master who's here about other races. But don't worry, my dear, I've also left some additional forces even Matthew doesn't know about. He is being well-watched," her mind-reading brother-in-law announced.

"Thank you. Was I that transparent?" Christine sighed.

"Frankly, Christine," Michael caught her gaze as he continued, "we all need to be on guard and I've pulled in a few more men from my former regiment to help us through the wedding and as long as we need them. Seems I pay better than the London hells where three of my former colleagues were. I found another working in his uncle's furniture factory. I have also learned loading furniture is not as thrilling as security duty for a Duke's household."

"What will you do after we get past all of this current craziness?"

"I expect," Michael replied, as he cut a glance at Cassandra, "with all the babies on the way, we will continue to need security guards."

"You?" Christine snapped her gaze to Cassandra beaming opposite her.

"Yes, oh, we're so excited. But with everything that has happened in the last few days, we were waiting to share."

"Oh, Cassandra," she grabbed her friend's hand. "I'm so sorry you had to hold your news."

"Nonsense. We have had a wonderful time sharing it within the household and that look on your face was worth waiting for."

"I assume that since my brother-in-law has chosen to say, 'all the babies,' you have deduced I may also have news?"

"My dear, you've been practically glowing since the wedding announcement." Cassandra leaned across the carriage and patted her knee.

"But we did such a good job of making it all about security and really it's still so soon to know for sure, I can't imagine anyone else really knows."

"They don't," Cassandra replied settling her skirts and shuffling her husband into place next to her. "I mean, I know because I've been around you these last weeks. But others don't know for sure. There's certainly speculation among the staff."

"I hate the idea of being speculated about. But I guess I deserve it. They'd know I haven't had..." She trailed off. She couldn't say that!

"Just so."

"Also, was it my imagination or did a person or two today avoid talking with me?" She recalled there were a couple of familiar faces. She had met some of the local social circle at Cassandra's wedding and the preceding bride visits. "But no one really even stopped us."

She had seen the looks, not quite cuts direct but several of the ladies had steered clear of her in the racing stadium stands. Gentlemen had nodded but not spoken to her.

She watched her brother-in-law's face harden.

"We aren't exactly sought-after companions either and it was a very raucous crowd. It could have been that or maybe some speculation," Cassandra mused to the carriage at large. "Very likely it will be as if nothing ever happened once you are married."

Christine noticed Cassandra seemed unconcerned with her diminished social standing now that she had married her footman. Clearly Cassandra's marriage meant more to her than any social status she might have had as the sister of a Duke.

Christine recalled her sister's delicate handling of the subject of an engagement ball too. Something about not needing to announce the wedding so formally since it was the holidays. Christine now realized it was because even a Duchess did not want to subject herself or her sister to social judgment. Just as well. She did not need to be popular.

As for today's cold shoulder treatment, since the wedding had not yet taken place she expected no one wanted to risk talking to her if she was unacceptably tainted but no one would risk censuring her either. Kathryn had been right. She would have been ruined by the swoon whatever the cause. She had had no choice but to be married, although she was not yet acceptable until the ring was on her finger.

Before she could sink deep into depressing thoughts, Michael pulled her against him. The excitement of the race, the press of the crowd and what was fast becoming confirmation of her state, morning-sickness which had turned into all-day-sickness for the first time had worn her out. That tiredness must have shone in her drooped countenance as well. Thankfully, the rocking of the carriage lulled her to sleep against her stalwart brother-in-law's shoulder.

Wedding Day. Her wedding! Had she ever dreamed of marrying a prince in a castle, and on Christmas Eve no less? She was quite sure she had not, and this was so close to the fairy tale as to make no difference. But the circumstances were not the same. She could not forget but for only a few moments at a time the reality of the threats against them.

While the week since the assassin's latest attempt on their lives had been filled with fittings, menus, decorations, obligatory visits and orders shuttled among their households, it had also been filled with security strategy sessions, hushed conferences she was not supposed to notice, and that anxious excitement tinged with uncertainty marking big events.

That they had decided to invite all the local gentry did not bother her. Being on display for fifty people she didn't know did not bother her. But she knew the rushed wedding held at Michael and Kathryn's house due to Matthew's poor circumstances bothered him. He had been edgy, distant with guests and even more protective than ever of her. No riding alone. Of course not. Have someone with you at all times when outdoors. Okay. No open carriages. The list of don'ts had grown exponentially each day. She was determined the over-cautiousness had to improve once she was living with him. Wouldn't it?

She determined this morning she would have to develop a system for getting down the stairs subsequent mornings to breakfast. The morning-sickness that had started the previous day never really left her but neither had she actually thrown up since just after rising from her bed. The roiling stomach was showing no signs of letting up even though she had steadied enough to get out of bed and dressed. And thankfully not throwing up again had allowed her to finally complete her toilette.

Indeed, experiencing the sensation of vomiting in the basin in her room had been an unpleasant shock. She could not imagine women had to vomit into bowls to then be emptied outside by servants. Poor things—both the lady and the maid. And of course, you could never hide a pregnancy from the servants under those circumstances. She imagined the dresses helped if you weren't throwing up, but...

She paused on the landing to settle herself. And that's when the hand snaked out to cover her mouth. She was pulled roughly against a large male body. She tried to bite the hand while his other vised across her body pinning her arms. She kicked at his booted shins to no avail. He shifted her in his hold enough to catch one wrist and wrench that arm painfully behind her back. "If you twist you will break it," he hissed in her ear.

He dragged her against the landing wall, hung with dark velvet curtains. She struggled against hard muscles, but the nausea she had previously beaten worked together with the man's slight body odor to swamp her senses. He did not even need to drug her for her to feel light-headed and disoriented. Fear rising with her gorge anchored her for just the moment she needed, however. She thought if she could pull the curtains down, she would leave a trail. Because she also knew if he was as skilled as he seemed to be he could get her out of the house undetected. With the last of her energy, she caught her left foot in the velvet and tugged. She heard the satisfying rip just as the vomit roared through her.

Gagging into his hand and retching from the gut, her spasms surprised her captor enough he loosened his grip. The grunt of disgust was her just reward as vomit oozed through his fingers, and onto the floor. She tried to make a sound but was too choked to be heard. And her triumph in puking on him was short lived as he slung his soiled fingers against the wall then wiped them down her dress. As quickly as he had grabbed her, he whipped a bandanna from somewhere on his person, wiped his hand once more on it and tied it around her mouth. The smell, the struggle, the lack of air overcame her, and she sank into oblivion.

"Your Grace?" Matthew looked up from his plate to see Christine's ladies' maid poke her head into the room and aim her gaze for

Kathryn. Kathryn motioned her over while the hairs on his neck stood on end. "Ma'am, I...I..."

"Go ahead, Beth. What's wrong?"

He and Michael and Jem were all pushing away from the table before she fully joined them in the room. "It's that there's a mess on the stairs, Ma'am." He knew, felt, something had happened to Christine.

"Tell us what happened." He heard the harshness in his voice and at the sharp look from Kathryn he evened out his features. But the tension rose inexorably.

"In truth, Ma'am, it looks like a struggle, on the landing." Before the maid finished, he was moving. He did not need to hear more. That she could tell there had been a struggle. That this past week had been too quiet. The assassin's death was surely known by now and his tormentor had time to replace him. That their wedding was today, and servants and tradesmen would be in and out of the house. It was the perfect time to slip in under cover of workingman's clothes and take her.

He reached the stairs and smelled the faint but distinctive odor. Had it been only a day since he learned she had begun being sick due to their encounter? That there was confirmation a child was on the way?

He took in the disheveled hanging and tracked the path they must have gone. The Duchess's floors were too clean for footprints, but he knew this house like his own. He found their trail in the hall near Christine's room, an empty chamber, readied for guests with just the faintest scrape of boot on polished floor. "Here."

"That's one of the rooms with the passageway," the Duke stated. "Let me follow it. She won't still be there, but I can gather clues. Jem, you hie to the stables. Ready the troops for the search."

"I'm going with you down this hall. I know she won't be there, but I have to see." Matthew noted his friend wisely did not reply. No one was stopping him from following her abductor's trail.

They charged into the dark passage, winding down ever-narrowing stairs to the cellar floor. "Stop, let's check for prints." He had the wherewithal to know what he needed to do. At least for now. "Surely we will find some."

"Here, a boot print." He saw even in the dim light of the space what Michael had found. The mark of an ordinary riding boot. Not a gentleman's but not a workingman's heavy boot. "There will have been a horse nearby."

Matthew's hopes of a trail rose as he spotted the churned path just yards from the door. "He left his horse right by the house. We never saw him, brazen bastard."

"We had people all over this area. I fear we will find at least one dead or injured guard." Matthew winced at Michael's grave pronunciation. Yes, one of Michael's people likely would be dead, another casualty of this war against him and his family. "Let's join Jem and the posse he will have assembled by now."

Without words, they raced through the Duchess's glorious gardens back toward the front of the house. He did not smell or see the blooms. He wanted his horse and he wanted his sword and he wanted to chop the swine who had taken Christine into small pieces.

Knight stamped in the forecourt, impatiently. Vaulting into the saddle, he swung the big head in the direction he had just come. He saw Michael speaking to a groom, no doubt sending a search party for the missing guard. He would someday make this up to Michael and his people. It would not be today.

The past few days in London had proved both illuminating and disturbing for Julian. The dead lowlife assassin he had tracked to a hedge tavern frequented by those plying the spy trade. That he had been part of Julian's past world did not surprise. What stood out was his connection to Herefordshire. Had this been a man grown up in the Village of Wilton? If this character was a local, someone pulling the strings was of their set, of the ton, or even of their neighborhood.

Manseri's words rang in his head...Duforge. His uncle. He spat the words. Could he be behind the attempts on Worley? *War is a wonderful cover for murder*. What did that mean? Was Duforge playing a double game? To take Worley from Matthew and claim landownership, then have Julian killed in the spy game and finally swoop in and claim to save the estate? And make some money in a side game selling secrets?

Pieces began falling neatly into place. Duforge was his closest living relative. If he killed Julian who had no living heirs, Duforge could argue to claim Weatherford for himself. Those types of claims had been made before and some had succeeded. Then he could use anything else he found in Julian's possessions to seed doubt about Julian's own service once he had access to Julian's remaining secrets. If Worley's property was truly available for the stealing, then Duforge would own not one but two estates—both Weatherford and Worley. United as one magnificent estate, they would be larger together than even Asterleigh's Hawthorne holdings. His uncle would command untold lands and riches. And all of the machinations hidden largely under the wonderful cover for treachery, the war.

Sebastian Drake must have known about this plan. He had probably seen the spy game as cover for the fratricide. Was this a case of hiding in plain sight? Let people believe you might be a spy so they spend all their time investigating the wrong endeavors. When they are embarrassed for not finding anything, the other crimes are too far gone.

Julian needed to get word to Michael Stafford. Duforge was not at his country home. Julian had checked on his way out of town. Duforge had not yet shown his face in London. He was somewhere, and he needed to be stopped.

10

---

*C*hristine awoke to the steady clopping of the horse's gait. She took slow breaths through her nose, stretching her senses to reach for any recognition of her surroundings. Outside, on a horse. She was quite literally slung across her abductor's lap. He was galloping but not at great speed. What did that mean? She worked to engage her brain. He was not worried about pursuit? He did not have far to go? Or a combination of both?

Other ideas, each less pleasant than the previous assailed her. Had he changed horses? Was he already far beyond the reach of her would-be rescuers? Did they even know she was gone?

Hard on the heels of those questions rose the most important question. Would Matthew know she did not run away from their wedding? She closed her eyes and opened her heart and she ...knew. Yes, he knew just as she would know. Their hearts were linked. They loved. What a wonderful time to realize her heart had known its mate. He would know, and he would come. With that comforting thought cloaking her, she sank back into oblivion.

"This way. He's ridden steadily since the stream." Matthew heard Jem call to McCaskill on his flank. Michael was further to his right with a small cadre of men. If their prey was not able to change horses, they would catch him in a few brief miles. If he went to ground, they would be searching the woods, farm houses, woodsman's cottages and caves scattered about this land. The tracks held firm and he wondered not for the first time if this was a decoy. Had someone else ridden hard in a different direction to distract them?

He motioned for Michael's posse to drift further to the right, deeper into Julian's lands. By his calculation, they had left Asterleigh's lands and were steadily crossing Weatherford. Soon they would plunge into the forest border with their Welsh neighbors, land untamed, unfarmed and littered with hiding places, lands into which he and his friends had rarely ventured.

He tried to bring back the map in his head of the untamed borderlands, the narrow section of land one of the earliest Lords of Weatherford had grown wild as protection against the unknown. Soon horses would be slowed to walking by densely forested pathless woods. He had to run down Christine's abductor before he disappeared with her into the unknown.

Where could he be headed? Julian's father had held expansive properties. Service to the crown had grown his estate many-fold and Julian had only added to it. He must have woodsmen, crofters, farmers, and all manner of tenants scattered across its vastness. Would one of the woodcutter's shacks be known to the abductor? Why else would he be riding to this location?

The path dipped sharply to the right and he saw it, something on the ground ahead. He slowed to observe a scrap of something out of place just on the path. From his perch he could see it was a slipper clean, new, not weathered. He checked, dropped to his feet, and swept up the shoe he was sure was Christine's. Tucking it into his riding jacket he motioned Jem's troop to fan out slowly on his left flank. Michael had already directed his men even further to the right. The grooms behind him had left several paces between them.

The paths had already become much less passable, but speed was no longer a concern. Christine had been brought this way and the villain could make no faster time than them. It would be only a matter of time his forces would find their target after all. He no longer believed there was a decoy. The distance traveled to place one shoe was too far and, in his experience, assassins did not work in pairs.

Other fears boiled to the surface, however. What was the villain going to do with Christine? Was he hurting her further? He had clearly already caused her untold injury judging by the altercation on the stairs. Was she afraid? Was their child healthy?

Hard on the heels of his fears for her safety were his fears for her too-strong spirit which might lead her to try something foolish, like escaping and running. And if she did, was that intended? What other reason would her abductor have for bringing them all here? Was she bait? Was someone else the intended target of this chase?

The answer came in a heart stopping whoosh as the scent of smoke came to his nostrils. Others smelled the fire and Michael's horse leapt in the direction of the blaze. And then many things happened at once so that all of time stood on a precipice for a moment, a moment in which two shots rang out.

The searing heat, the instant loss of control. By some miracle he did not go toppling from the saddle, but he lurched forward, causing Knight to check and the rider behind him to veer. Then the explosion of the tiny hut's flames over its roof pushed Michael and his group back from the small clearing they had just discovered and at the same time, through pain shrouded vision, he saw the staggering form slumping to the ground yards ahead.

Then, he forgot about the heat in his arm, the danger of the flames, ripping free of the stirrups and vaulting himself forward toward Christine. Pulling his riding scarf over his nose and his hat tight on his brow he raced for her, sliding low across the leaf littered ground to avoid the flames and any more bullets.

Scooping her limp form, he staggered some yards into the woods. He wanted cover for her and he needed to check, to know. Shaking, he placed his lips at the pulse point of her throat and felt the throb of the very real beat of her blood.

Dimly he heard the voices, battling the flames, shouting orders. In a haze of smoke and pain, he felt a firm hand touch his shoulder, then they were there, taking her, reaching for him.

Christine clawed her way out of the flames, the smoke, the heat burning her stockinged feet. But the heat was easing? Air, she could breathe and arms, not his, not that foul body odor. Matthew's arms? Then the new harsh smells brought her fully awake. She smelled blood, felt the warm flow down her arm, the side of her dress. Hers? Whose?

"There you are, my dear?" A voice, she recognized, not Matthew's. She blinked. "Christine. We are so glad to see you." Michael.

"Fire," she breathed the words, tried to see.

"Yes. I want to check you, don't try to move."

"Matthew?"

"He's here. Hold still." She pushed against Michael's hold and heard him mutter. He helped her sit. She blinked, wiped her eyes and saw Rose bent over Matthew's slumped form next to her. "He's going to be okay.

"I want to see him. What happened?" She shifted to lean against her injured fiancé who was clearly alive but not yet speaking.

"A bullet went through," Michael told her. She gasped. "He's lost blood."

She watched through now-focused eyes as her body-guard Rose tied off a neat bandage on Matthew's arm. "You okay?" she whispered from a dry throat and parched lips.

"I will be, when I know...you're okay."

"I am, though I won't lie, I feel very much like I've been run over. You, stay awake, please."

Matthew watched as Christine faded again, slumping back in Michael's arms. He wanted to be the one to catch her, but his head swam. Christine's guard, Rose, had been tending to his wound which hurt like the devil but was thankfully no longer oozing blood. So when Rose offered his hand to pull Matthew to his feet, he could only be grateful for Rose's strong grip as his legs steadied under him. Feeling like an hours-old colt, Matthew took several breaths before he loosened his grip with the stalwart guard.

He saw the fire had consumed the cottage and men were battling small clumps of flame that had jumped into the surrounding leaf litter. Matthew was so weak, he leaned against a tree and contemplated then discarded the idea of joining in.

Something pressed to his palm. He looked down at the flask, twisted the cap and took a long drag. "Keep it, you might need it on the way back." Matthew stared at his best friend and for one of the very few times in his life let Michael Stafford give all the commands.

The riding party that thundered into the forecourt at Hawthorne mid-day on Christmas Eve was much the worse for wear than when they had left. None of them had been able to determine how to get all of Matthew's blood off Christine's gown. Her sister would swoon at the sight. It could not be helped, and for his part, Matthew did not have the strength to solve the dilemma.

As if the women were conjured by his musings, Cassandra burst from the door flying toward them, Kathryn hovered more decorously on the threshold. "She's alright. It's not as bad as it looks," Matthew said before they could begin their questions. He would gratefully let Michael deal with any hysterics.

"She's drenched in blood. I'd say it looks very bad."

"Cass, it's not hers." Michael's low tones checked Cassandra's accusations. Michael jerked his head toward Matthew. He saw the moment Cassandra realized he had been the one injured. She promptly shut her mouth.

In front of this crowd, Matthew was determined he would not fall off his horse. He swung his leg over, held tight with his good arm and steadied himself. He took deep breaths until he was ready to proceed. Following Michael into the house, Matthew and others of their rather motley-looking troupe surged into Kathryn's private parlor at the end of the hall. He sat, while Michael laid Christine on the settee against him. Matthew's tension relaxed as he found her hand and squeezed.

"I don't really need an explanation...yet. But I think you both need Dr. Bridelsby. I've sent for him." Kathryn eased onto the settee at her prone sister's hip under the watchful eye of her husband.

"Michael, I've also sent round to the neighbors that due to a small fire and the subsequent disruption, the wedding was delayed until this afternoon. Two hours hence."

"Today." He heard Christine's whispered words to him, her sister, and the room at large.

"Yes, my love, today," the Duchess confirmed. "I knew you would not want to change it, but I was sure we wouldn't make it this morning. Convenient of you to stage an actual fire to make my story the truth."

"Got out. I wasn't supposed to die, unless he got lucky. I was the bait. Shot Matthew," Christine rasped.

"I did notice the mess the two of you made of yourselves. Got yourself shot, huh?" The Duchess turned an understanding gaze toward him.

"All those years the French didn't manage it and I take a ball in my own neighbor's woods." He laughed, they laughed. Such was the power of Her Grace of Asterleigh Kathryn Ragland Stafford, to charm and comfort.

"Why didn't he kill Christine?" Matthew mused aloud to his closest confidantes. He was relieved to be able to speak freely once the ladies had departed to see to his betrothed.

"She was the bait. He needed her alive." Matthew winced at Michael's blunt assessment.

"But she could be carrying the heir." As Matthew said the words aloud, the pang hit strong and sharp. *His heir, their child.* He heard Michael's blunt reply through the roaring in his head.

"She's not your wife though so no one is the heir until you marry. Worley's the target. The bullet was intended to kill, and if the bullet didn't get you, bleeding out might. Or the fire."

"You're a cynical devil, Michael." Matthew shifted to try for a position that would accommodate his bulky bandage. The throbbing pain in his arm was robbing him of his ability to think rationally and he needed to sort out this latest mess and ready for a wedding.

"He knew he hit you." Colin had stayed quiet during that exchange his words drawing all eyes to him. "But he didn't stay around to see if you died. Could we use that somehow?"

"No!" Matthew was emphatic.

"No?" Asked Colin.

"I promised my betrothed I was marrying her today and I am marrying her today. Just...later today," Matthew was beginning to hurt all over.

"Very well," said Michael once more the epitome of the Duke.

"Then we will make sure there's a damn wedding."

If ever there was a wedding party more injured, ill, on edge and anxious Christine could not imagine. She knew weddings were supposed to make you jittery and nervous, but she could not really conceive when a bride had had a kidnapping ordeal, her groom had been shot in the rescue, a matron of honor was bedridden, and several members of the wedding party had other various burns and injuries. Christine's wedding would make monster brides stories from her former time and place look like walks in the park. "If you don't stop wiggling miss, I'm never going to get this strand threaded."

"Sorry, Beth. I'm nervous and my stomach is roiling and..."

"You should have let me get you that willow bark tea."

"I don't need anything to relax me. It would probably have the opposite effect and I'd end up drunk." She heard the sulkiness in her own voice.

"You're going to have to have something in your stomach or we won't be able to be sure you get through to the end," Beth declared.

"You sure are cheerful."

"I'm not the one insisting on going through a wedding service after being brutalized and not eating a thing."

"I'll try some toast if you insist."

"Oh, Christine, look at you." Cassandra swept into her room in a flurry of blue satin layers. Christine had decided Cassandra would wear blue, Kathryn green and her own dress would be a soft gold. She had flatly refused to wear white even though Kathryn assured her it would not be gauche. To her mind, it would be totally inappropriate, and the simple, flowing gold gown looked beautiful with the plain gold band Matthew was going to put on her finger. All would coordinate well with the delicate cross on the thin chain he had given her that he said he had saved from the depredations of his family's fortune. Her gown and her attendants would look lovely with the candles and the season's greenery as backdrop.

"I have been sent to inform you that Kathryn has been held prisoner in her room until the start of the wedding, so she has instructions for you."

"Beth is lecturing me about eating, so get in line."

Cassandra stepped in behind Christine and regarded her in the dressing table mirror. "Just gorgeous. You're a veritable golden goddess."

"Thanks. That's good then because I will need some divine assistance to make it through the service standing up." Christine sighed and leaned into Cassandra whose hands had come to rest on her shoulders. "By the way, have you seen Kat eat anything? She looked very pale earlier."

"I believe Michael spoon fed her some broth himself. He has deputized Ellie to keep Kathryn to her bed and even from that position she says I am to inform you the guests are arriving and to give me Matthew's ring so I can take it to her."

"I'm almost afraid to ask, but I want to know...has anything gone wrong?" At Cassandra's puzzled look, Christine laughed and corrected herself. "Wrong this afternoon I mean, anything else?"

"Ah, no, thank goodness. Matthew is here pacing Michael's study." Cassandra fluffed at Christine's dress and studied her pale face in the mirror while she relayed all of the afternoon's goings on. "The food has turned out lovely except one pie which got forgotten in the hullabaloo of the fire. Cook has made some nice tarts to replace it. Oh, and of course," she continued almost without a breath while fussing with the small details of Christine's person. "The story of the fire is all the buzz. Again, thankfully we really didn't have to lie about it. And, Matthew is having trouble sticking with his role of the injured in the fire story though it is something of the truth."

"He was injured and there was a fire Hmm...good one," Christine pronounced.

"And you are having a terribly bad day of the babe. Everyone is a little scandalized we're talking about it and a little jealous." Cassandra added that little detail Christine could have lived without knowing.

"Do we really have to tell people that? For the ones who don't know yet, can't we leave them in blissful ignorance?" Christine groaned but noticed at the same time her toast had arrived magically. Christine really did not know how Beth managed it, but she took the warm buttered bread and nibbled only to be caught up short by something Cassandra had said. "And you said Jealous? People are jealous of an American who's having to have a rushed wedding?"

"Well of course. After Michael, Matthew and Julian are the hottest prospects on the marriage market. Now there's only Julian left..." Cassandra laughed.

"You forgot Colin. What about him?" Christine took a bite of toast under the stern eye of Beth.

"I guess you're right. But he's not a Lord so..." Cassandra trailed off to study Christine who began eating at a faster pace.

"Well, I'm still embarrassed about the timing of everything, but Kathryn assures me once I'm married my little indiscretion will be largely forgotten," Christine at least no longer had to worry about appearing pale. This discussion had more than reddened her cheeks.

"Oh yes, your child's pedigree will be one of the highest in the land as the son of a Baron who is a major landowner and also the relative of a Duke. Oh, or daughter. But, enough of that, I see you've finished your toast. We should go."

"Here, miss, don't forget the gloves." Beth shoved the pair at her as Christine hurried to the door. She hesitated at the opening, realizing the toast had hit the spot and steadied her. "Thank you, Beth, for taking such good care of me. You are coming down?"

"Yes, thank you, miss. And I did get the package you left for me. It is the loveliest thing I have ever owned. I will be proud to wear it. And I will see you next when you are ready to get out of that beautiful dress." Beth turned back to the dressing table to tidy Christine's things. She had to trust that Beth would indeed feel comfortable coming to the wedding in the lovely new dress they had given her.

She had been saying the wedding rhyme over and over in her head. "Something old is the cross, something new is the dress, something borrowed is, well, a lot of things right, including the gloves? What is blue again?"

"Oh, your garter. We need that lovely blue one they made for you for wearing and throwing." Cassandra turned just as Beth picked up the piece of lace from the floor. Both of them had to help her lift the froth of skirts and slide the spare garter into place. The effort cost her some of her recently found steadiness.

"It's going to be a miracle if I get to the altar without having to be carried. I feel sick again."

"Maybe this time it's just nerves and seeing Matthew standing there waiting for you will help. I'll make sure Michael knows you may be holding on tight," Cassandra announced.

"Just so he doesn't literally have to carry me."

In the corridor, Christine met her dashing brother-in law and her stunning sister. She noted Michael had positioned a chair for Kathryn and was staring sternly at her, presumably so she would not consider moving until her turn to walk down the aisle. Dimly Christine heard the strings play a familiar tune. She had not been sure which one would actually signal her to march but once Cassandra smiled brightly, sent her a wink and started for the aisle, she found her mental place in the service. Michael reluctantly released Kathryn who straightened her spine, pinched first one then the other cheek, took her bouquet from a hovering Ellie and blew an air kiss to Christine, then she whispered as she began to move. "You're where you belong darling,"

When Michael turned back from watching his wife and held out his arm, Christine wondered to whom he was beckoning. An English Duke decked in his finery, the king in his castle, was going to escort her, Christine Ragland down the aisle to marry a 19th century English Lord. What a fabulous dream.

"Do you Matthew Dalton Anthony, take this woman, Christine Mary, to be your wedded wife?" Through the haze of pain, of the cloying perfumes, the loud smell of flowers and greenery, some un-fresh bodies, he heard the words, dimly. He believed he responded appropriately, except when he was asked to take the ring. He was staring at Christine, her moist eyes and over-bright cheeks, her pale neck and sweat-beaded forehead. He was seriously concerned she would topple over any minute, his hold on her hands not enough to keep her upright.

And his arm burned like the very fires of hell. He feared moving it in almost any direction, would tear any of the stitches that talented little maid of the Duchess had sewn into his arm. Bleeding wounds did not figure into their Weatherford fire story. Nor really did fainting brides. She was not supposed to have been overly affected by any of those activities.

When the Vicar allowed him to kiss the bride, he brushed her lips, then slid his mouth to whisper in her ear. "Only a few minutes and we will get some air."

"I may make it, but it will be close."

He smiled at her, at the life she represented, lives actually, his future, his helpmate and friend. She was such a treasure, a gift packaged in gold as she was on the eve of the time of year of the greatest gift. Through all of the trials of the last weeks and months, she was the bright light. He was eternally grateful she had come into his life.

11
———

*H*e had not expected to be nervous on his wedding night. Clad in his dressing robe and trousers, he stood at the window of the sumptuous guest chamber he had been given adjacent to Christine's, his heart pounding uncomfortably. The rushing of his blood made his wound all the more painful and he wondered how he was going to live up to either of their wedding night expectations especially since he likely could not use one of his arms. He shook his head at the thought. His bride was unlikely to be up to much wedding night activity anyway. Surely together they could muddle through.

But he didn't want to muddle through. He wanted to make this night memorable for her. So he squared his shoulders and took a breath, then tapped on the door and pushed it open soundlessly.

He needn't have worried about disappointing her. She was curled on her side on top of the silk counterpane fast asleep. He moved on silent feet toward her bed and stared down at his sleeping goddess. What a treasure he had found in his hayloft that fall day. Strong, beautiful, small, and so very capable Christine. And like her elder sister so very fragile.

When he settled onto the bed beside her, she stretched and slid her fingers across his leg. He pulled her shoulders onto his lap and stroked the flowing tresses of mahogany hair. "Mmm...must have dozed off. Promise I'll wake up."

"I'm afraid you will have to darling if you want your Christmas and wedding present, Lady Worley."

"Oh, that sounds nice. Hey, I have Christmas and wedding presents?"

"Actually, just one present. For this year only, it's just one. I think you'll be pleased."

She stirred, brushed her mass of hair back from her face and looked at the wrapped package he held out. When she reached, he jerked it back eliciting an aggrieved laugh and a tussle. She snatched it away, sitting upright surprisingly fast to rip the plain brown paper he had covered it in. She studied the packet long moments, then untied the ribbon holding the leather pouch together, fingers visibly shaking. She opened the packet and smoothed the contents flat on the sheets.

"Matthew?" The look of confused awe on her sleep-flushed face was one he would never forget. For this one moment in time alone he would always be glad he gave her the gift. "Matthew you can't, you said..."

He touched her lips with one steady finger. He gazed into the beautifully stunned, disbelieving orbs. "I have, and I can, thanks to several things that have happened including the generous dowry Michael gifted me for you on our wedding."

"I had a dowry?"

"Apparently your brother-in-law established one for you. He had already signed the funds into my name. He would not consider taking the money back."

"Wait, that's still..."

"Stop arguing. He's yours. From the moment he came into this world, I have thought of him as I do you, as an immeasurable treasure. I want you to have him, and I am intensely grateful we do not have to sell him. I will be able to enjoy watching you train him."

"That's the other thing. You were sure you'd have to sell him. My dowry wasn't the only thing that happened then?"

"No and it's a complicated tale about unraveling the past that has taken the greatest edge off the burden of debt. But that story is not for our wedding night my lovely new wife Christine Drake, Lady Worley."

He had given her the colt, his most prized possession, the foundation for the rebuilding of his fortunes. "Stop thinking. I can see your questions running through that lovely mind of yours. It's time for me to enjoy you a little."

"And that's another thing. I...I don't have anything for you."

"Of course you do. When you gave yourself to me, I got a wife with whom I am exceptionally pleased and now we have a coming child. Those are all the gifts I need."

"And there is that dowry too."

"Ha, yes. But I didn't marry you for that."

"Sneaky of Michael to figure out how to give you money you couldn't refuse."

"Yes, if I could have avoided it I would have but I do believe he is grateful you are here with us and as safe as we can make you. His priority is Kathryn, and by extension you, the child, his sister and her family, his estate, and his friends. He has a lot of worries so I believe he is happy to share them with me."

"I expect we will find many additional servants magically moving to Worley with us to help with that safety."

"Oh, yes, Rose and McCaskill will be following you wherever you go."

"At least until we vanquish your enemy."

"At least. But enough talk this of unpleasant business. Tonight, I want to enjoy my beautiful bride."

"Mmmm...I believe I am fully awake now."

She turned her face to his and smiled. She traced the curve of his lips with her fingers. "When I saw you in the portrait," she kissed him, just a brush of lips, "I was so taken with the way you looked." Another kiss, deeper, longer. "I imagined what you were like."

She climbed onto his lap, slid her gown up her thighs, straddling him. When she kissed him again, he closed his eyes and leaned back against her pillows, pulling her more fully on top of him. He dug his fingers into her bottom, his wound clearly all but forgotten.

"You were so much more than I dreamed," she murmured then took a breath. "I didn't imagine the cleft just there." She touched her lips to the indention in his chin, then trailed them down his neck to the wildly beating pulse point at its base. "So much stronger..."

He lifted her then more fully onto his lap and she felt the evidence of his need. Reaching between them, she made short work of the flap of his trousers, driving them both higher with deepening kisses. She sank down, impaling herself on him. "So powerful."

He awoke on Christmas at dawn with his arms full of warm woman. Stroking down the lean planes of her back, he reached for the soft globes of her tight bottom. He shifted, opening her and drove them both once again into oblivion. When he returned to his senses, the servants were stirring. He knew no one truly expected to see the newlyweds at breakfast but his bride would want to check on her sister and he would want to hear that no mischief had happened at

Worley in his absence. He suspected Michael would have a full report for him.

He disentangled from the silken limbs draped over him, slipped from the cocoon of her bed, and found the chill water basin and shave soap someone had thoughtfully left in his dressing room. He had most surprisingly slept soundly. Safety and the favors of his gorgeous wife were clearly good for his health.

Clad in clean clothes, with a neatly tied bandage and freshly shaven he was feeling quite remarkably refreshed as he entered the breakfast room. "You are up and about rather early for a newlywed, are you not my friend?" Michael said.

"Well, I'm a newlywed on Christmas morning and I've always been up early. This is a slovenly hour for me to emerge."

"You can be forgiven, of course." Very much the Duke, Michael gave an almost indistinguishable nod to Hallthorpe and the room's other occupant and they disappeared. "I expect you are anxious to know how fares Worley?"

"You know me well." Matthew shook his head, a rueful acknowledgment of his dire circumstances.

"Jem sent a rider this morning. All was quiet. Even villains take Christmas off I assume, and I expect he knew we would be even more vigilant during the wedding."

"I'm grateful for small favors. And how fares your bride?"

"Kathryn has had trouble sleeping through the night, so I, too, am grateful she was able to sleep in this morning. I expect she was thoroughly done in yesterday."

"She organized a beautiful day for us. I can't quite believe it but I was able to see the lovely flowers and recognize the quality of the exquisite gown Christine wore and so I appreciate her efforts on our behalf."

"She is pleased. More than pleased, she is relieved Christine is here."

"Have I told you, we talked about their...travel here?" Matthew remembered to tell his friend.

"No, what does Christine say?"

"She told me about the painting. I'd like to see the one Kathryn brought with her. We need to figure out if there are others. Is anyone following them or worse, if they find one here will it take them back?"

"That's brilliant and frightening at the same time." Michael frowned. "I've been so focused on keeping her away from the painting that I haven't thought about others and what they might mean. Come, it's in my study."

The small portrait of Michael and his first wife was quite similar to the one Matthew kept in his study of him with his horse, in its size, and familiar brush strokes. "This is done by the same artist as mine. I'd go bail it's a series. I just thought mine was a gift, remember?"

"Lady Weatherford."

"Yes, didn't she paint these for our families?" For Matthew the pieces were falling into place.

"We each have one and somehow in the future the paintings must have been organized into a collection. Julian's and Colin's portraits are probably still in the shop. The same store near their homes, correct?"

"That's what I recall Christine said. The question is who's next?"

"There's the one of Julian she painted just before he disappeared into France. I don't recall the setting of Colin's. But that doesn't help us figure out who might be next," Michael mused.

"You know, I don't think it's about one of us. It was about them, actions they took. Someone is probably looking for the sisters and she's going to choose a painting when she traces their steps. And then if the steps hold, the store owner is going to send one home with her."

"Of course, all of that depends on someone knowing them well enough, caring about them enough to look. And they haven't mentioned any friends or relatives they are close enough to for anyone to follow," Michael recalled. "Kathryn was solely focused on finding Christine. She never acted like there was anyone else."

"It's just as likely a stranger may be next, or no one. Who's to say for sure anyone else is drawn to the pictures as the sisters were? And the real question is do we really want to know?" Matthew voiced these thoughts and was prepared to go bail they were in for more surprises from the future.

"Good morning." Christine pushed the closed breakfast parlor door more fully open. Peeking, she saw her husband and brother-in-law deep in conversation and no servants in sight.

"Come in, my dear. Happy Christmas."

"Merry Christmas to you too, Michael. And Matthew, happy first day of marriage."

"And to you, lovely lady. Are you well?" He had risen and pulled out the chair next to his. She subsided into the chair without taking any food. "I can see you are not all that well. I will ring for tea and toast."

"Maybe just toast, and a little water. I made it down but ughh."

"Can I help you into the sitting room, to lie down?" Matthew asked with what was a very nervous expression.

"No, I'd like to sit up. I think I'll be all right. Just give me a few minutes."

Both men were staring at her as if she might cause a mess right on the breakfast table and she also realized she had interrupted their very private conversation. Well, she couldn't help it now, nor could she get back up for a while. Not until everything stopped rolling and pitching inside her and the room stopped moving.

"I believe if our mother had been alive she would have told us that the Raglands and the Powells had very difficult pregnancies. We both might have taken better care."

She had meant it as a joke, but as she saw the very hurt expression cross Matthew's face, she realized she had better quickly backtrack. "I'm sorry," she said as she reached for Matthew's hand under the table and squeezed. "That was in very poor taste."

"Nonsense. You and your sister have had great difficulties. You see we men are not offering to trade places with you, only to be supportive."

"And you are, and we thank you for that." She was smart enough to retain her husband's hand to continue to soothe his wounded pride. But she turned to Michael. "And how is Kat this morning? She's not down yet it looks like."

"No, I believe she was sleeping in, for which I am grateful. She has been very uncomfortable at night and has not slept but a few minutes at a time."

"Poor thing. Should I go up and check on her?"

"When you are able to do so. For now, you can eat that toast." Her brother-in-law adopted his sternest expression.

"Hey, how did that get here?"

"You did not see Hallthorpe. He is a man of many talents." Michael smiled.

"Clearly."

"Actually, I think it appeared while your eyes were closed, and the room was spinning," her new husband chided.

"You could tell it was that bad, huh?"

"You were practically swaying. Michael and I were petrified we would have to catch you before you fell over and cracked your head."

"I'm thinking if you carry me up, I can sit with Kat, maybe have some more toast with her. And tell her about my wonderful present."

"Present?" Michael raised his eyebrows.

"He gave me Night Sky for a wedding and Christmas present. I'm still in shock."

"Ah, lovely. You will be very good for that colt."

"Thank you, my brother-in-law. And by the way, there's more I need to thank you for, but I can't really think very straight right now. Matthew if you'll take me up to be with Kathryn, you can get back to your secret plotting conversation."

"Us, plotting? Hmmm..." Matthew smiled, released her hand and stood to do her bidding. And definitely looked guilty of plotting.

"Big sis. Can I come in?" Christine peered around the door into her sister's lovely sitting room. She had stood outside for a few breaths to steady herself and noticed the quiet. Scanning the room finding no one was there, she tiptoed to the door to the Duchess's bedchamber, tapped softly and turned the knob. Her sister lay on her side, eyes closed, with her leg supported by pillows. "Kat, are you sleeping?" she whispered.

"No. My eyes are closed but I've been awake a while."

"I'll keep you company then. Turns out, I'm not much good for anything in the morning still but conversation."

"Can you climb up here? Or there's a stool..." Kathryn gestured to her dressing table area and Christine considered.

"I should be able to, thanks. Oh, Merry Christmas."

"You too. I'm so glad you're here." Kathryn had infused so much into that one short phrase, Christine's heart beat pounded, and she wanted more than anything just to comfort and entertain her sister.

"Compared to last Christmas. What did we do? Remember the scrawny tree?"

"Yeah, and we didn't thaw the turkey enough." Christine boosted up on her sister's plush pillows and took Kathryn's hand.

"And look at us now. I've been here eight months and still some days I wake up and wonder where I am or when it will all just dissolve back into my former life."

"I hope that will go away. I can't really imagine going back, leaving this behind, or even worse having the baby and him not knowing his father, me not being with Matthew."

"And same for me about Michael. It shouldn't be possible should it? Not now that we seem to be exactly where we belong."

"True. I couldn't imagine when I got here how I'd fit in. But the more Matthew needs me, and then the baby and how much you need me..."

"You cannot know what a relief it was to me for you...well, we've said it before, haven't we? My heart was so broken over you and so full of Michael at the same time."

"Now you don't have to choose or to feel guilty." And that thought Christine was the most comforting thought she could have given her sister. All in all a good morning's work.

The soft knock on the door preceded Ellie. "Good morning, Your Grace. I've some toast and a message from His Grace."

"Let me guess. 'Stay in bed.'" Kathryn said it with a pretty accurate imitation of his lovely English accent.

The maid chuckled. "Not far off, ma'am, but he actually said their Lordships would get some business done this morning then if it suited, they would join you for Christmas lunch up here in your apartments."

"Do I have a choice?"

Her maid laughed fully this time. "No, ma'am, you don't. But Hallthorpe found some more greenery and he and Miss Cassandra have sorted it out to make your sitting room look quite festive. And I do believe there are presents."

"So Cassandra came over?"

"She did. Just to check on the two of you. She and Mr. Jem are keeping watch at Worley." Ellie declared while also bustling about Kathryn's chamber.

"I hate for them to be alone," Kathryn said.

"I don't suppose they're all that alone with him working all the horses and her organizing the house. And they probably like being free to come and go," Ellie replied.

"True enough. Now, Ellie, I understand there's an English tradition for presents to be given to the servants at a celebration in their quarters. I'm sorry I won't be able to do that."

"Ma'am, it's a present every day for me to be here. I never dreamed of a job like this. It was going to be village seamstress for me, if I was lucky. And my sisters, too."

"Well, I want you to have something. Will you bring me that package on the dresser?" Christine watched Ellie's cheeks stain as she carried the bundle back to Kathryn who stayed her hands.

Christine was intrigued. Kathryn had managed to sneak in a present without her eagle-eyed maid knowing. She always had been a Christmas surpriser-extraordinaire. "This is for you and your sisters from me and my sister."

Ellie's strong, slim fingers shook as she pulled the ribbon. The paper fell open revealing ...fabric? "Oh, ma'am, look at this." Her awed tones saying clearly, she had not owned anything like it before.

Ellie spread out the first cutting of a pretty yellow fabric. To Christine, it looked like a muslin. As the maid separated the folded lengths, she revealed five different fabrics and a small package with various ribbons, buttons, threads, and lace. There must have been enough fabric and decorations to make five new, very pretty dresses. Her sister spoke as the maid separated buttons and bobs. "I thought of all the dresses you have sewn for us, and that you all should sew some for yourselves. I know there are assemblies in the village."

"Yes. We will feel like the belles of the ball in the gowns we make from this gorgeous fabric," Ellie replied, her voice reflecting her joy. "Thank you, thank you so much."

"My pleasure. You have been both a friend and protector to me and my sister and we appreciate all of you."

"I'm speechless, except for I can say 'thank you.'"

"Oh, and there's one more thing. Please take this," and she pressed something looking suspiciously to Christine like rolled hills into Ellie's hand, "and take your sisters home to spend the rest of the day with your family. Clearly my sister and I aren't going anywhere."

"I will wish you Merry then and won't argue, although His Grace will want me to report in we're leaving. I'm sure he will assign someone else to watch over the two of you. But I thank you again, Your Grace. We all thank you."

Christine squeezed Kathryn's hand and watched her sister subside back onto the pillow. No, they would definitely not be going anywhere if giving presents tired her out this much.

The Christmas season must have been, in some twisted way, sacred to their villain. They passed the days into the New Year in relative quiet, enjoying the colt's progress, repairing, and refurbishing Worley and visiting with the Stafford's who were completely homebound and welcomed any distraction. They played cards—who knew his new wife was a card shark? She and her sister taught them games and there were many ha'pennies lost over the card table that had been placed in the Duchess' sitting room.

Michael was loath to venture more than an hour's ride from home so the messengers between Hawthorne and Worley and from Hawthorne to London were busy. Somewhere in the pleasant haze of the holidays and the quiet new year, the message arrived from Julian with the grim details that his maternal uncle could be their villain.

He did not know this Duforge, at least not to recognize him in person. And as Julian had said, he was neither at his country home nor to be found in London, so Matthew was not sure how they would fight the man. Who knew how many resources he had at his disposal —lethal human resources.

Christine had also been correct in her assertion there would be many more servants in his household now she was resident. The extra maid in their chambers remarkably resembled her lady's maid. He expected Michael had brought in another one of the Primble sisters whose job was clearly not just hair and clothes but eagle eye security. He could not fault the man for his over protection. They had been fighting villains together for too long to let down their guard and Michael would want their flanks covered.

The military contingent had also grown, and he caught sight of one of the regular perimeter patrols they had set up on his grounds. His horses were finally safe from the tampering as there were more hands in the stables, even some whose job was as guard only, and they were all armed to the teeth. He was quite sure no one would be able to sneak in as there was no longer any time when the horses were unattended.

He pondered the new challenges the new year would bring. He would see, and he would be as ready as he was able.

12

*P*ounding somewhere on a door woke Christine up. As she focused her sleep-fogged brain, she heard hurrying feet coming her way. Something was wrong. *Kathryn.*

"Ma'am, ma'am...wake up," Beth called into the room then discreetly shut the door.

"I'm awake. What is it?"

"It's Her Grace," came the muffled answer from the other side of the door. "Rider from Hawthorne, says it's labor this time, powerful." Her husband was also rolling out of bed. Once the door shut to his dressing room, Beth hurried in.

"Alright, books, bag, I'm wearing the breeches."

Her maid held out the pants and turned away. Christine looked down at the slim fitting riding pants and the time it would take to get them on, ultimately tossing them aside. "Something sturdy, doesn't matter what it is."

"This blue will do. You won't need to change again at Her Grace's. I'll be coming, too, if I can make so bold. You and Ellie might need me, especially if the doctor's not there."

"I assume Michael sent for the Doctor, too?" The question was rhetorical. The doctor would have been fetched if he was in town. If he wasn't at home, he couldn't come, and Christine was on her own. She was going so it didn't matter whether she was going to be the backup or in the lead. She and Beth moved in tandem down the stairs and swept into the main hallway just as she saw Mrs. Soggs handing Matthew his greatcoat. She heard the scrunch of carriage wheels and realized that riding her own horse was very likely no more until after her own baby came. No point in arguing and January in England was freezing anyway.

Her regular posse was in attendance and they galloped ahead as the carriage rocked into motion. She tried to order her thoughts. How far along was Kathryn? The baby was due mid-March, and this was the third week of January. Maybe seven weeks early? It would be tiny. They would worry about lung development and eyesight. Or everything would be fine. They would stop the labor and the baby would wait a few more weeks to be delivered.

If the baby was coming what did she need? "We're going to be in time," Matthew said.

"Sorry?"

"I said, we're going to be there in time for you to help." Matthew squeezed her hand and gestured for her to lean against him. He must have felt her shivering from the cold inside the carriage and the fear for her sister.

"I hope so, but I had jumped ahead to all that needed to be done. Maybe because I'm thinking it through, not that much will be needed. All will be fine, and we can be on our merry way." She heard the brittleness in her voice and tried smoothing out the grimace on her face.

"Having known Kathryn since she fought off murderous villains, survived being shot and charmed the entire village, I am confident she will weather this storm as well."

"I'm worried about his size and how we will know what's wrong."

"How do you know it's a he?" She turned to him and saw the twinkle in her husband's eye, returned the squeeze of his hand and snuggled deeper into the warmth of his tall form.

"Of course, it could be a she. Can you imagine what Michael will do with another Kathryn?"

"I imagine he will spoil her mercilessly. She will be horrible, and we will have to keep our own child away from her because she will be a terrible influence." His mocking tone soothed her as she knew he was trying to do.

"I somehow think it's a boy. And I have a name I hope they use."

"Oh...what is it?"

"William. It's a family name."

"And you don't want that name saved for your own child?"

"I actually think it belongs to the first born." She looked up once again at Matthew. "I imagine you have some wonderfully strong names in your family you'd like to use."

He turned to the window, flicked open the curtain with his free hand and said, "Sebastian."

Of course. Perfect. Sebastian. She interlinked their fingers and they rode the remaining few miles of road in silence.

Hawthorne's lights were blazing, the front doors open wide and grooms milling on the gravel ready for their arrival. She almost didn't wait for the carriage to stop but was down the steps the moment they were flipped open. She didn't stop to greet Hallthorpe but bolted for the stairs. Several things struck her at once as she charged into Kathryn's bedchamber. Ellie, setting supplies on the nightstand by the bed. Michael sitting next to Kathryn gripping her hand, a very built-up warm fire, and no doctor.

"Kathryn, who said you could go into labor in the middle of the night on the coldest night of the year?"

"I...didn't...plan...this," she gritted out. "Can you...make it stop?"

"Let me see where you are, I will know better. But looking at Kathryn's shape, the rock-hard mound of her belly and the time she estimated had passed since Kathryn was coming down from the contraction they witnessed, the baby was coming. As she feared, the top of the baby's fuzz-covered head was visible. "Kat, we're gonna do this now."

"Now...okay. Little sister, you can do this...with...me, I...know."

"I can do it with you." All of a sudden it was very easy to give orders. "Michael, go ahead and sit behind her, elevate her shoulders, give her back support. Ellie, cloths, scissors close and I want you right here."

The maid moved to stand behind her left shoulder. The covers had already been strategically untucked and extra toweling covered the silk sheets. Michael had doffed his boots and was positioning himself behind Kathryn as instructed. As the next contraction built, he gripped Kathryn's hands and she arched into his chest.

"I think it's okay to push during this contraction if you can."

"I-I-I-ahhh...can."

Christine lost track of time as Kathryn's contractions were followed by labored breathing by moments of rest for her sister. At some point, a glass of water was pushed into her hand. Beth. Now she understood why Beth had been brought along, to tend to her!

Kathryn's mottled face dripped sweat, strands of darkened hair glued to her cheeks. Michael had discarded his neckcloth and waistcoat. She was as hot as those two and while the morning sickness had given way to a more manageable state, she was sagging. She could not keep up this pace for hours and she knew Beth would see and report to Matthew who would step in and take charge of her.

She did not know what they would do when she was forced to take a break. Maybe the doctor would make an appearance in the meantime. She could hold out a little longer, but she could also ask if help was on the way. "Where is Dr. Bridelsby?"

"On holiday," Michael bit out. "Visiting his daughter in Kent or somewhere as far away as possible."

"Sounds like we're the team then," Christine announced cheerily. "You've had a little break. I'm going to see where we are." Just as she positioned to check her sister's progress, all hell seemed to break loose.

"I...think...it's coming...nooowww!" The scream was accompanied by the squirming whoosh of a tiny child into Christine's arms. Ellie pushed the cloths at her and Christine stared down at her amazingly small but otherwise perfect looking nephew.

"It's a boy, Kat. He's tiny but beautiful." She turned him over to clear his airway, and wipe his nose, all the while Ellie was swiping at him with a cloth to clear the goo from his skin. Christine did not have an accurate estimate of his weight, but she could guess, and she would after she got over the rush of catching him.

She also was amazed that he was barely as long as her forearm. Seconds seemed like minutes as she waited for his first wail, but once he started, he was loath to stop.

Ellie had a clean fresh diaper rolled and together they sorted it out around his doll-sized bottom. She also had other duties to see to Kathryn and she decided the baby's screaming gave her perfect cover to take care of Kathryn and be sure all was well with her sister. Human babies were smaller, but their messes were quite as difficult to clean up in the 19th century as those of horses she decided. She was immensely grateful Kathryn and Michael had eyes only for their son because Kathryn would be mortally embarrassed at this part of giving birth. She used some of the clean cloths to tend to Kathryn and also cut off her soiled clothes under cover of the sheets.

They had made no clothes for a baby this small, so the ever-resourceful Ellie used the scissors first to cut the umbilical cord, then to cut the hem off a perfectly good dressing gown. She shrugged at Christine who wanted very much to laugh.

The very-outraged miniature person in her arms continued to

scream as Michael slipped from behind Kathryn, lifted her sister more fully up onto her bank of pillows and wiped the sticky strands of hair from her face. Ellie handed him a clean cloth he dipped into the basin and stepped back to her side to wipe the sweat from Kathryn's face and neck. His sharp eyes tracked Christine's own movements as she surreptitiously examined the baby. She estimated he couldn't be more than three pounds and 17 or 18 inches long, but he looked ...fine.

The Duke, the army officer, now new Dad reached his arms to her and she placed the fussy child in his waiting grasp. The look on his face almost made her weep. "Hush, little one, we've got you," he whispered. Amazingly, or maybe not so amazing, the baby's wails gurgled to a stop.

Michael turned toward Kathryn whose eyes were all for her two men. Christine intended to give them their moment, but she had to know that one more thing before she stepped out. "What are you naming him?"

"I thought William if it's okay with you," without taking her eyes off the baby, Kat rasped as she accepted the precious bundle from her husband.

Behind her, Christine heard Ellie tidying up the bed. She watched Michael subside at his wife's side and reach one long finger to touch the tiny, wrinkled face. She was mesmerized by the tableau and a little lightheaded from all the excitement.

"It's fine with me. It's perfect, in fact." She heard Ellie open the door to slip from the room, turning to join her. She took a first step forward and a second and then she felt it, the wave of dizziness swamped her. Before the world went black, strong arms caught her.

"I'm sent by Her Grace to see how the lady is." Kathryn's maid peered into the dark room that had been Christine's just a few weeks ago.

She was ensconced once again in the bed he and his wife had enjoyed on their wedding night and all through Christmas. It felt familiar to Matthew, but he dearly wanted to be at home, his home, with his wife.

"You can tell Her Grace that her sister woke a little while ago and had some of the Cook's special broth. She's sleeping again but all seems to be well enough."

"Very good. Beth was planning to come up, spell you a bit so you could eat. His Grace was going to come down to the dining room as Her Grace was going to...well, that's improper to share is it not? She's going to have some privacy, so His Grace was looking to see if you would like to join him at the table."

"I'd be glad to move from this chair if Beth will stay." Matthew stretched and sighed. "Ellie, thank you."

"It's our pleasure for such a tough lady. She was terrific this morning. I know she did it on hardly any sleep and no food."

He was not sure he was up for conversation. He was not steady. Even now, he shivered at the thought. Had he not been waiting in the hall for his wife immediately outside the Duchess's rooms and Ellie not warned him Christine looked done in, his wife would have swooned and possibly been injured hitting the floor. She was not getting stronger. She should be.

He'd fumbled through the conversation with the Housekeeper. She had understood his questions and answered frankly. He now feared Christine would have as bad a time during her indisposition as the Duchess. How he would manage a swooning and headstrong wife with all the other problems plaguing him he did not know. And he was not in the mood to be lectured by his longtime friend if that was what this summons was about.

"Matthew, how fares Christine?" Michael stood as he entered the dining room.

"She's asleep. Beth is with her." He eyed the food spread out on the sideboard and while his stomach was growling he was not particularly interested in food. He sat and took the wine poured for him by Hallthorpe. "I believe congratulations are in order, my friend."

"Thank you. I'm still in shock. He's small but he looks fine. He is fine." Michael shook his head then just started laughing. "Matthew, my son is here and he's healthy and my wife is healthy. It's a damn good day."

"To their health." He held up his glass. Yes, he could agree it was still a good day.

Three days had passed, and he still had not moved his wife home. Riding back and forth to sleep with her then rise at dawn to leave her to work with the horses and return late in the day was wearing on him. And she was his, his responsibility, his partner and he could darn well care for her here at home.

He was determined today would be the day. The report was she had sat up most of the day and eaten well. Surely she would be up for a short carriage ride. He was going to be there when she woke from her afternoon rest and ask. Or demand. Or maybe both.

"Hunter, will you saddle Knight and Fleur. You can join me on an afternoon ride."

"Yes sir, whoopee." As the boy dashed off, he spied Rose striding toward the stables. He turned at the scrunch of gravel as the carriage rumbled up. Out of habit, he ducked his head inside to ensure there were no booby traps.

The chill wind lashed his face and he and his horse flew effortlessly over the lush fields. Hunter followed on the little mare. She would be grateful for the run. He knew the carriage rumbled far behind. But the sense of freedom today, of riding before the wind cleared his head and helped him think. He had needed to make plans. The holidays and the health scares and the birth had slowed his plans. It was time to find a permanent jockey and to enter another race, and to apply to join the guild.

He thundered into the castle's forecourt. Let the household hear his arrival he thought grimly. He was here for his wife. Hallthorpe's minions had the doors open and his old friend stood just inside the foyer. "Good news, you've arrived in time for tea...with your wife."

He ignored the amused look on Michael's face. His eyes were all for Christine. She looked well, rested, rosy. "My dear."

She reached for him as he entered. He touched his lips to her cool hand. "You are looking well. How are you feeling today?"

He sat next to her and kept her hand in his, turning it over and linking fingers. "I feel better. I guess I was just dehydrated, and it got me. I just had to sleep it off...for three days."

"Yes, I believe you didn't wake up when I slipped out in the mornings. We will have to be sure none of that happens again. After you have had your tea, I have the carriage coming. I hope you will be up to the drive home."

"Oh yes, please. I've missed...you. And, If it's okay, and won't delay you too much, I'd like to check back upstairs. See the baby, check on Kathryn."

He smiled at her. The look in her eyes was all he could have asked.

"Of course. I will pay my respects as well. Let me know when you are ready to go up." He knew she saw through his excuse. He was not letting her climb the stairs by herself. "Then, I've got some business with Michael, but I will be ready when you are."

Extricating his wife from her sister's orbit and from the baby who he had to admit was engaging, took longer than he had planned. Afternoon was gone by the time their procession rolled up to the front doors of Worley. Christine would be tired. He hoped, prayed, she would rest so he could get some more work done without having to worry and watch over her.

Then from the corner of his eye, he recognized the horse being led around to the stables. Of course, he had not been lucky enough that Christine also had not recognized it. When they gained the foyer, his wife hesitated. "I will leave you to your guest. If there's anything concerning me, you'll share?" Her raised eyebrows were enough to tell him that if he balked she might try to intrude.

"Yes, my dear. Are you going to rest? Staggs can escort you."

"I could use my most English accent and say, 'as you wish.'"

"If only," he muttered.

"What was that?" The twinkle in her eye belied the stern look on her face.

"Hmmm...yes, I will see you shortly."

Negligently sprawled by his fire with the morning's worn newssheet, Julian Thornton's pose, nevertheless, said clearly, he had news. Matthew shut the door with a click. "Good evening, my friend."

"And you. You look like you could use a brandy. I'm enjoying a drink at your expense."

"Thank you, yes, I will join you." As he walked to the decanter Matthew pulled the cord and was answered by Mrs. Staggs. His worthy housekeeper would be the best source to report on his wife's whereabouts, he settled behind his desk.

"So the fair Lady Worley has her sister's tendencies to insert her dainty nose into the business?"

"She's just as bad. But, maybe this indisposition is a blessing. She has not felt up to following me." He scowled at the loud guffaw from beside him.

"I'm sorry to laugh at your misfortune but you did ask for it my friend."

"Alas and I did. When are you going to fall into parson's mousetrap?"

"Not until I am bound and gagged into it I believe."

"A wise friend once told me, you would not have control to avoid it once it found you. I believe that. It seems I would give my life to protect them. And that brings us neatly around to your visit. What of this business?"

Matthew listened with growing certainty that Julian was right about their enemy. But if he was not at either of his known locations, how would they find Duforge and rid themselves of him, before the villain had another assassin in place?

"I've sent inquiries to contacts and I have reinforcements coming from London."

Matthew looked his question. "Some useful employees."

"The very best. We will be ever-vigilant."

"That was so exciting...are we going down to congratulate him?" Christine said.

"Of course, if you're up to it," Matthew replied.

"It seems adrenaline makes me feel terrific. Knight won. Oh, he will be so proud of himself!"

"And you know this, how?" He smiled fondly down on his beaming wife.

"Remember, I am the horse whisperer."

"Ah, yes, one of your many talents." She leaned against him then, took his arm tighter and he led her through the thronging crowd toward the winner's circle. He also watched the people, the hands, the jockeys. Anyone could be the villain's next assassin. He did not for a moment believe Duforge would miss the opportunity to attack in a crowd such as this.

And Julian's men had arrived some days earlier. Julian's guards were trained to protect someone whose identity should not be known to the outside world. If Matthew had not been shown the men protecting him and his wife, he would not have been able to pick them out.

He would worry about their enemy, but he was also determined to enjoy this victory. The small guild held prestigious local races and this one included a couple of Welsh horses and one or two from Scotland. Winning was not only lucrative but would help him build his reputation. "Worley, a moment please."

He turned at the hail from the tall, slim gentleman, dressed comfortably in the guise of country squire. He also knew Mr. Markley to be a shrewd stable owner, and president of this local group of owners. "Mr. Markley, well met."

"Yes, that was an impressive performance. I understand you have only begun racing that horse recently?"

"Yes, sir, that's correct. Actually, he was on campaign with me. It wasn't until I hired on special talent that his racing acumen was specifically cultivated." He turned to Christine and raised her hand to his lips. Then he looked directly back at the gentleman. "May I present my wife, Lady Worley?"

Speculation flared in the shrewd grey orbs on level with his. What exactly the gentleman saw in the tiny, obviously blooming, beautiful woman at his side he could not say but it was clear the man understood his meaning. Ladies, generally, did not work with horses. There were a few noted exceptions, but "ladies" certainly did not do so publicly. That his wife might have hidden talents would fascinate this horse aficionado.

"Madam, may I offer my sincere congratulations to all of you on the race's results today?"

"Thank you, sir. It is extraordinarily exciting to be here today." And he watched her move to Markley's side. "Tell me, sir, it is acceptable for us, including me...to go down and congratulate Knight?"

Markley offered his arm and assured Christine she was welcomed to join their horse. And as neatly as that, Matthew's treasure had made another conquest. There was just something about her manner, how she regarded one that made one want to be near her. He could not say which one characteristic it was that won people over, whether it was because she listened so intently or because her warm drawl was mesmerizing, she was just simply a light that people wanted to be near. Lost in contemplation of his wife's charms, he did not realize the separation that had formed between them.

The jubilant crowd was spilling from the upper rows into the public aisles, owners mixing with local spectators and a man was making directly for Christine. Then another pair of men crashed into the interloper, knocking him back. They neatly tripped over each other, then clasped shoulders as if jolly and drunk.

Matthew surged toward the man, now falling back into the crowd. He wanted to catch him and to find out who sent him, or even better to track him back to his master once and for all. He spotted one of his own guards, nodded at the fast-disappearing back of their would-be assassin and passed him off to the former soldier-turned protector.

Julian had obviously witnessed the approach and had melted into the crowd up ahead. It was no doubt his men had thwarted the suspected killer. That the man had attempted a public assassination suggested their villain was becoming desperate, and that his pursuit of Christine had become obsessive. It was time for drastic action.

"As you can imagine, we found no trace of him. I think one of my men could describe him but that will do us no good. He is completely ordinary."

"Wonderful. An ordinary-looking assassin with the boldness and skill to attempt killing in broad daylight." Matthew was angry and frustrated as he paced the small keeping room where they would meet with Markley and discuss admission to the prestigious group of owners who ran this track. He couldn't think about races when he had just watched a man attempt to stab his wife literally in the back.

"We will get him my friend," Julian said. "An obsessed man becomes careless. Today, he was very careless. He would have known she was well-guarded, and he never would have gotten too close."

"Well, he got too close for my nerves."

"I know and I'm sorry about that. But my men were right there. They would not have let him make a move. And he may not have even realized who they were. I hope not at least. We should still have the advantage of some cover."

"That is some comfort but not enough. It's time we acted."

"Yes, we need a new plan."

13

$\mathcal{M}$atthew didn't like it. Neither did his friends. Their grim faces said as much, their poses stiff with the ticking of the grandfather clock in Michael's study the only sound as they made the decision to lure their villain out with bait.

Christine was feeling much better. She had been walking in the sunlight, meeting him at the rails during the afternoon exercises and visiting her sister and the baby. If they were being watched, the villain knew her capabilities. He would know she had been venturing out, heavily guarded but still living in public. How they were going to use Christine's apparent re-emergence into daily life, shield her from any real danger but convince Duforge to make a move would be difficult.

"My dears, we are so glad you could join us," Matthew said. They had all risen at the arrival of the ladies and Matthew motioned to the open seat next to him. When the Duchess settled into her customary seat by the big desk and Christine had likewise subsided by him, Michael laid out their plan. He watched their faces. The Duchess eyed her husband speculatively, and Christine stared in amazement.

"You would actually consider the appearance of letting her be captured or shot at or whatever might happen." Kathryn's words were the same as those bandied about the room for the last hour.

"If we establish a pattern that looks like we're trying to avoid a pattern he will believe we are still being vigilant. But he should be able to decipher our system. He may not be lured into striking, but I believe by the time we actually spring the trap, we will have her far away from the danger, but with a chance to get him."

The knot in Matthew's gut tightened at his own words. He could not believe he was even considering letting Christine be involved, but the idea of waiting for the next attempt sat equally as heavy in his gut. They had each been shot. They had suffered the two fires, a recent knifing attempt and all the other times they had probably thwarted were too many to name. The odds they would miss the next time...well, he just wasn't a betting man.

Christine shifted her body turned toward him fully. "Thank you for trusting me enough to let me help. I will follow instructions and we will come through this with flying colors. You'll see." Then she smiled brightly at the entire room.

"I was afraid she'd say that. Your wife has too much courage by half." Julian straightened and leaned his elbows over his knees, catching Christine with his dark gaze. "This will require your willingness to do exactly as we say. There is no improvisation in spy games. Do you understand, My Lady?"

"I do. And for all you don't think we know what is going on, I realized what happened at the horse park. You know we do have eyes. We can see when you get upset, and then there are all those little hushed conversations. And I recognized your men. Well, I should say, I recognized one of them. The other was very well disguised. Oh, and If I didn't say it already, thank you for saving my life, Julian. Now, back to our planning."

"Those two you recall, and several others are going to be involved in this mission. We can't introduce you, but I will try to make them known to you, so we can be sure you at least know who is friend."

Her week had been organized into a pattern of sorts, with rotating visits to her sister that almost made sense, mingled with walks with her husband or Rose and McCaskill. She still could not quite believe she was being allowed to participate in this attempt to lure the assassin or the actual villain out to attempt to kill her again. She wasn't even afraid for herself. She was afraid for Matthew because for all she had thought they were using her as bait, she knew he was really the bait. That he was joining her occasionally in her "public" appearances, she knew he firmly believed the villain was watching him. And trying to find a time when he was most vulnerable. To her mind, it would be when the two of them were furthest from the house, on foot. On the walks. She might be the one shot at, but like with the fire, she knew he was the one they wanted dead.

She believed it was more than just the heir and the land and the legacy. There was more to this villain's animosity. She and Kathryn had determined the villain still had scores to settle from the war, from losing his position and fame, and Sebastian Drake and by extension his brother the lauded cavalry captain, were to blame. Of course, Julian was also to blame.

She and Kathryn knew Duforge would have special plans to try to ruin and ultimately kill Julian because of all of them his spying had been the most direct threat to Duforge's position. From all she learned, Julian had brought down central figures in Napoleon's government, his personal inner circle and he had actually affected the outcome of at least one battle. She was sure their man was out for more than just money. He wanted revenge.

"The roses are going to come back. And I understand we might have some jasmine." Christine ambled under the arch where a gardener had been nursing the precious climbing rose back to life. She had decided something else that afternoon. She had known the villain would not be happy with her death alone. She had determined, because of his obsession, this almost-declared love marriage she had would be out in the open once and for all.

"Will you sit here with me?" Matthew looked around. She knew he was checking for vantage points their assassin could use. She had chosen the bench well. It was protected on three sides by the hedge and the roll of the land. Only their fronts were exposed, and it was not their villain's style to try for a head-on attack. "Sit down, I won't bite."

"Sorry. I remain concerned of sitting outside, but this is a lovely spot." When he reached for her hand she grasped his tightly and turned toward him. "Something is missing from our marriage and I want to fix it. Do you remember our vows?"

His face had paled, and she hurried to reassure him. "Remember when we said 'love, honor and cherish?'"

"Yes, I recall we had to leave out 'obey.'"

"Well, of course. But it was—is the 'love' part I want to talk about."

"What about it?"

"We don't say it to each other."

"Of course..."

"No. We don't. We haven't. We need to start. Unless it's not true for you, then I will understand."

The shot came from the front. It slammed into her and she toppled over the back of the bench. He dove for her. Dimly he heard voices, running, shouts, shots. All hell broke loose. He did not really see any of it. He just saw her on the ground with a hole in her dress.

His heart had stopped. He was sure of it. All the light went out of the day, the world. The earth stopped spinning as he lay on the ground with his wife, his love, limp in his arms.

He put his ear to her chest and felt...nothing. He slumped over her.

"Ah, you have made this too easy. Duforge said you had gotten sloppy," the whispered rasp mocked him.

He heard two more shots fired almost simultaneously. He expected the searing burning. It did not come. He must be numb. His wife was dead, and so must he be. He could not feel pain. "My friend, you are okay?"

"Okay? Julian, do I look okay? My wife is on the ground. He dragged himself off her and glared at Julian and he was ...grinning?

"My Lady, you were magnifique. What an exquisite plan. You will need to stay there a bit longer until we are sure there are no others. This one is clearly dead," Julian whispered to her in her prone position.

Matthew was staring at his wife's chest and the hole in it. The hole from which no blood oozed. Then she winked at him. Winked? "Shhh. Play along until Julian gives us the all clear. You could wail a little."

"I am going to wail on you alright when I learn what you have gone and done you little fool."

"Just pretend to be grieving, please, for a little while. In case Duforge is watching. We know he might be. But now we have an advantage. He thinks I'm dead. He may be back someday. But today is a good day."

It took several hours to sort out the mess of the dead assassin and to enlist just the right servants to help them put on the charade of the shooting of Christine. By the time they retired to her sitting room Matthew was thoroughly exhausted and totally furious with his wife. She was dancing a jig.

"We did it. We have him convinced he shot me. When you go into mourning, he will have gotten his revenge on you. Julian and I believe he will move on to trying for Julian. And he's ready."

"What I want to understand is how you knew they would try for you in the garden just then."

"Kathryn and I had realized there was a lot more to the Duforge saga than just money. Pride and revenge were at stake. Punishing you was part of it. Getting to Julian, ruining Sebastian, all were part of his egotistical plan. And I knew he was watching us. Julian realized he would know we were baiting him, so we decided to try to find the time and place he would be least likely to strike and lure him then. When I could be wearing an armor plate and position myself in front of you."

"And the garden was the time and place, why?"

"The safest place, the one place where he wouldn't try."

"I cannot imagine how you thought that through, but I believe I'm grateful. Angry and grateful. Now, tell me how I am to go into mourning over you?"

"Easy. I don't get seen outside, and that's not a huge burden since I'm not doing all that well anyway. You wear black and act all broody and mad and the servants put up the black drapes. We play it out for a while to see if we can get Duforge himself back into the area to gloat over your misery."

"What a sick and twisted mind you have. I'm grateful it's being employed to my benefit." She had dropped her gown and was cinching a robe over her pregnant belly. The small roundness made her even more exquisite. The benefits of having a home bound wife were beginning to play in his mind. He knew she saw his eyes narrow.

When he reached for her silk clad bottom she climbed into his lap and kissed him lavishly. "About our conversation this afternoon. I do love you, you know that, right?"

She leaned back and looked at him. "I believed you did, or I wouldn't have given you my virginity. But I did want to hear you say it too."

"I love you, My Lady, my life, my partner. And I love our child." He placed his hand on her belly as he returned her kiss. When he surfaced, he thought of one more thing. "We are going to have to keep you trapped in your room. Whatever will we do in here for the next days and weeks?"

"I'm looking forward to finding out." She slipped her robe off her shoulders and pressed her glorious body to his. Then she whispered, "I'm glad you became the Lord of my dreams." And she kissed him again until he forgot all about villains and murder and revenge. He wouldn't have a long reprieve but for that night their dreams would be only of each other.

EPILOGUE

*H*e expected her. Not her exactly, this long-legged, red headed, pistol-packing virago, but someone. Lord Julian Thornton, Earl of Weatherford had been both literally and figuratively pulled into the dreams of two of his closest friends with the arrivals from seemingly nowhere of their fated loves.

Now just weeks after the marriage of the second of those women to his closest neighbor, that another American woman should arrive in his life by way of his mother's artist's eyrie did not surprise him. That she was a runner, a badge-carrying officer of the law, fallen right into his arms just as the threats to his life and land were becoming more than he and his friends could fight alone, Julian knew was not coincidence. Fate had been generous.

Ella Anne Catherine Cannon had a canny sense of direction but this morning she knew she was not where she belonged. Following the cold trail of two missing Alabama women, she had walked in their footsteps only now to find herself somewhere out of her own time altogether. Palming her piece and drawing the string tight on her loose sleeping trousers, Ella slid off the low sofa on which she had awoken in a crawling crouch and crept toward the sound. In a stream of morning light, a gentleman lounged against the wall by a pretty window seat.

"There you are, I've been waiting for you to wake up."

THE END

~

Don't miss out on your next favorite book!

Join the Satin Romance mailing list
www.satinromance.com/mail.html

AUTHOR'S NOTE

Watch for the third story in the Dreams series, *Earl of Her Dreams,* in which the handsome, mysterious half-French Earl meets his match in a transplanted lady detective who is just the person to help him vanquish the enemy who has plagued them all. We will alert you on "OliviaRitchRomances" when that story is coming!

Finally, I wanted to give credit to another author for the idea of sawing off an arrow. Indeed, the act of sawing off arrows came from the author of a favorite American Western romance series I've enjoyed although the circumstances surrounding the arrow being loosed were certainly different.

— OLIVIA

ABOUT THE AUTHOR

Olivia lives in Birmingham, Alabama with her handy husband Henry, their cats and dogs. When she is not writing, or reading romance, Olivia works full time for a non-profit, travels to watch her college-age children's track meets and squeezes in an occasional three- or even six-mile run.

www.facebook.com/oliviaritchromances

ALSO BY OLIVIA RITCH

WITH MELANGE BOOKS & SATIN ROMANCE

Dream Series

Duke of Her Dreams

Lord of Her Dreams

Novellas

Room in the Inn